CONTENTS

TO SIT, UNMOVING

by SUSAN STEINBERG

A MAN GRABBED my father by his shirt. Then he punched my father's face.

My father fell backward into the street.

The man stooped in the street to my father. He pushed his fingers into my father's pants pocket. He fished out my father's wallet. Then he ran.

This was on the island. Puerto Rico. In the city. San Juan. On a street in the city. I don't know which. But the street was a low-lit street. And nothing was open on the low-lit streets that late at night but bars.

My father couldn't tell much of the man. There was a ski cap he said. A dark coat he said.

The fist before it reached his face.

What else, I said.

I mean I would have said.

I mean you would have said had you been sitting at the table in my father's office the following morning.

What I mean is had he been your father.

But there was nothing else.

My father fell backward into the street, his hands moving up to his eyes.

* * *

In the city were wild kids shooting up. Hookers poking from doorways.

This we heard from the man with the mustache who stood at the desk in the lobby.

The concierge, said my father to me and my brother, and he said it slow like, con-ci-erge.

The hotel limo wouldn't take us to the city. It would only take us to my father's factory and to other hotels that looked like ours. But my father said that this was stupid, that we were from a city and big deal this one he said.

I'll rent a sports car, he said. A red one, he said winking at my brother who lay on his side on the lobby floor.

In the city were wild dogs. Low-lit streets.

The concierge pulled his mustache in a way that looked like it should have hurt. But his mustache looked fake and I knew my brother would piss his pants if I said this.

You'll get stabbed in the city, the concierge said looking at me. He pulled on his mustache, and to my brother I said, Look, and pulled on the skin above my lip so it looked like it hurt. My brother laughed and rolled onto his back.

My father said, Stabbings. Big deal.

Stabbings, he said. We've got stabbings at home.

We had shootings as well. My brother and I heard shots at night from the park.

People walked over my brother and my brother tried to grab their legs.

My father said, We're from Bal-ti-more, and made his hand like he was holding a knife, ready to stab.

The concierge said, There are private restaurants here. In the good parts, he said. Keep to the private beaches, he said.

There was a Chinese restaurant in the hotel lobby and the inside looked like China. The Mexican one looked like Mexico and the music in each was different.

The lobby stores sold watches and gold chains and suntan oil. They sold American papers and American drinks. We liked the American drinks. We were Americans, and in America, or the States as my father told me and my brother to say, we drank regular drinks. We did everything regular in the States. We weren't stuck in the States in a dull hotel.

We could walk after school to the city park. We could walk home alone at night.

My father threw some dollars to the desk. He said, Sports car. Red. My brother thought this was funny. This, because my brother's brain was wired wrong. He wasn't retarded. But his brain told him to do things other ways. Like sometimes it told him to laugh a lot. Sometimes it said to be silent. There were days we could poke and poke him in the ribs and he still wouldn't say one word. Those days he wore his headphones. He listened to metal and my father said, You'll rot your brain.

My father nudged my brother with his foot. He said, Get up, son, and my brother grabbed my father's leg.

The concierge spoke Spanish on the phone. We knew he was talking shit about us. We were white, as if you didn't know this. We were stupid white fuckers. We were rich white fucks.

This is not anger. I am not angry.

We sat nights, my father on dates, in the hotel room. There was nowhere else to go. We could play on the sidewalk outside the hotel just until it got dark. Just until the concierge shooed us back inside. At nights the lobby stores were closed. And we were not allowed on the beach. Dangerous kids hung out on the beach after dark. The concierge said, Do you want to get killed, and my brother made a gun with his hand and said, Pow. Nights we ordered room service and charged it to the room. There was American food on all the menus. We ordered from the American side. But it all tasted weird and Puerto Rican. The hamburgers came on regular bread. The potatoes were bananas. The TV shows were all in Spanish. Only some words were English. Chevrolet. Golden Skillet. My brother laughed at the cartoon commercials. There was one for chicken, one for something else. A drink.

To say my father was an inventor would be to lie. He mostly invented things that didn't work. In fact, only one thing worked, and you couldn't call someone an inventor when he invented only one thing that worked.

It would be to say I was a killer because I had one murderous moment one night with some kids in the park.

It would be to say my brother was a genius because he had one good

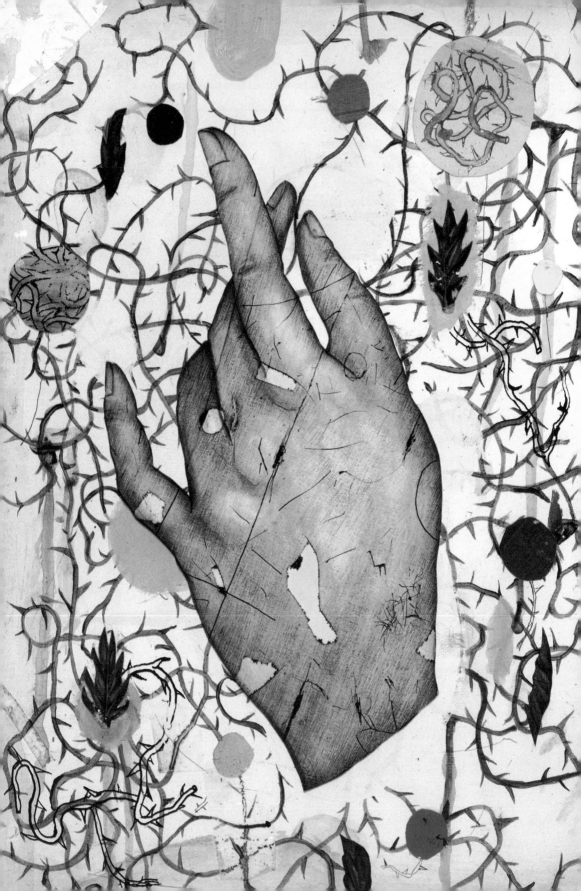

idea, just one, once, slamming into the soft walls of his rotted brain.

The things my father built that didn't work were kept in boxes in a room in our house in the States. I never knew what these things were supposed to do, but there were wires and powders and pieces of foam in boxes, always, in this room in the house.

When he invented the one thing that worked, some filter that clicked into some kind of mask that factory workers would strap to their faces in order to breathe, he took me and my brother to California. A celebration. My mother was dying and couldn't go. I mean she was literally dying. My father said, You could use the air, but she said, Go, to my father and went back to sleep.

My father took us to a restaurant that overlooked a city. Los Angeles, I think, but we were so far up on the top of a hill it didn't matter what city it was.

My father called the waitress darling. He held her by her wrist. He ordered a bottle of wine. Three glasses, he said and winked at my brother. He talked about things we didn't understand. He said his filter could take dust from the air. It could crush the dust to smaller bits. The waitress laughed and said, I don't get it. She walked away.

People want to breathe, my father said. I'm an inventor, for the love of God.

My brother drank his wine like it was water, and my father said, Easy, son.

He smacked the table. Do you hear me, he said.

My brother looked up.

Not you, said my father. Your sister, he said. She never listens.

Below us the city's white lights blinked. It could have been home, how it looked. It could have been me and my brother dusted in sand, high up in the city park.

My father said the waitress was a dog.

My brother looked about to laugh.

A toast, said my father.

We raised our glasses.

To dust, he said.

Dust was mostly human skin. I learned this in school.

My brother barked at the waitress.

My father touched our glasses with his glass.

* * *

When the man in the coat and cap ran off my father rose to his knees. He must have looked like he was praying. Or like he was drunk. Motionless, touching his bloody face. Struggling to stand while holding his nose. Then the blood between his fingers. Dirt on the knees of his pants.

No big deal, he said.

He could wash the pants.

And he had nothing in the wallet.

A couple bills, he said.

And the wallet was a cheap one bought on the island.

His license. No big deal.

You can replace a license, my father said. They give anyone a license on this backward island.

Even the ladies, said my father.

He was with some lady, a date, in the city. She worked in my father's factory.

He said, She's the best-looking one. Her hair. It's danger.

Hot to fucking trot, he said.

Before the date, he took me and my brother for a ride in the sports car around the hotels. The tires squealed. My brother screamed when the car went faster.

My father said, That's right, son. He said, This is the life.

He stopped the car outside the hotel. He said, This is your stop. He said, I've got a date. He said, Hot to trot. He slapped my brother on the back. Be good, he said.

We were in his office the following morning. My father had spent the night in the office. He had called us before he went to sleep. He said, I'm working late. Go to sleep, he said. But we watched TV instead.

In the morning the concierge knocked on the door. He said, Let's go. We would ride in the limo to my father's factory. The limo was better than the sports car. We could see out the windows of the limo, but no one could see us in it. People always tried to see inside. Kids pushing their bikes up the street. Ladies in cars beside us. When I gave them the finger my brother laughed.

There were plates of eggs and fruit on a table in my father's office, but we didn't eat. My father had two black eyes, a blood-crusted nose. His words sounded thick and slurred.

He said, I was barely out of the car and this guy he grabbed me. He punched me. I fell backward to the street. And my nose was bleeding like hell.

He and the date were getting some drinks in the city.

I'm allowed, he said.

He said, Isn't that right, son. He looked at my brother who looked at the silver pitcher on the table. The pitcher curved inward then out. On the inward, things looked upside-down. My brother and I liked to look at ourselves in the pitcher. We looked wild and snake-haired and monstrous.

It wasn't a pitcher you put things in.

My father said, Don't touch the pitcher.

He said, Touch it and die.

He was looking at me.

Five hundred dollars, he said, it cost me.

Keep off it, he said.

I didn't touch it, I said.

You were about to, he said.

My brother couldn't look at my father's face. I had to look.

My father said, A knuckle sandwich. Pow, he said.

He nudged my brother and said, Pow.

My father said, She liked the car. Of course she liked the car, he said. They all like the car. She turned everything on. The radio. Click. The heater. Click. He said, Click click click, and looked at my brother to make him laugh. Click, he said and poked my brother in the gut.

My brother got up from the table and sat on the floor.

My father said, A son of a gun.

When the filters filled with dust they were trashed. Then the trash was poured into landfills. And landfills were full of rats. My father should have known this. He went to school. He should have known about landfills. And about rats. How these rats had very sharp teeth. How they could find the filters in the landfills. How they could chew straight through the filters.

You're crazy, said my father.

He said to my brother, Your sister's crazy.

My brother laughed.

But I knew dangerous dust was released by rats.

It became a part of the air again.

My brother wasn't retarded. He just couldn't learn right. His brain made things backward. Like his right and left. And telling time. And he couldn't tie shoes. He wore slip-on sneakers. The kind with the Velcro. They always looked crooked, too big for his feet.

It's a phase, said my father.

He's a genius, he said.

But my brother and I knew better. His brain was our secret. Only he and I knew how truly fucked-up it was.

My father said, It's because of your mother.

She was sick, then dead.

But that wasn't it.

The masks were sewn in a factory on the island. The factory was small and made only masks. Bigger factories made the filters. These were in Baltimore and I had been to these factories with my brother. They were big and full of workers working big machines. The workers were men who smoked while they worked. No one talked. They didn't like me and my brother running around. We tried to push buttons on the machines when the men weren't looking, and my brother would squeal like a fucking retard and the men would say to my father, Get these kids out, and come walking at us in a slow monster way that made my brother squeal even harder, and I was the one to tell the workers to get back to work, and they laughed at me, like, Who the fuck does she think she is, but they knew who I was.

At some point they would be working for me.

We all liked the island factory better. The workers on the island were ladies who spoke Spanish and played with my brother's hair. My father went to the island over the summers. It used to be he went alone. But now he had to take us.

Weekends we stood in the ocean. We collected snails in a bucket and raced them on the sand. My father slept on a chair. We put snails on my father's feet to make him jump. He said, What the hell. He didn't shave on the weekends. The ladies around him laughed when he jumped.

There were crazy kids who climbed the palms. They picked coconuts and split them up with a knife. They sold them one for a dollar to me and my brother. They told us we were stupid fucks. They said, They're free if you climb the tree. Neither of us could climb a tree with no branches. They said we were rich white fucks. We already knew this. The boys didn't wear shoes or shirts. They're free, they said. But we gave them the dollars.

My father called the kids the Coco Locos.

He said, Keep away from those dirty kids.

We went weekdays to my father's office. It had a glass door. On the other side of the door was the factory. We could see the ladies hunched over their table sewing masks. The ladies couldn't see us in the office though. The door was like the limo windows. I liked to be on the unmirrored side. Though sometimes I couldn't help it. Sometimes there were limos with other people in them. And I was with my brother on the mirrored side. We were playing on the hotel sidewalk. And I wanted to look in the mirror. But I knew better than to look too hard. Even my brother knew someone could be giving the finger.

When the ladies used the mirror to fix their lipstick, my father stood on our side and said, Stupid estupidos. Sometimes he opened the door into the ladies. Sometimes he said something funny like, Working hard I see.

The ladies took breaks from sewing masks. There was pan de agua and coffee. They prayed before eating by closing their eyes and moving their lips.

They're devout, said my father. De-vout. Good ones, he said.

I had heard my father ask the ladies to dinners. Lucky you darling, my father would say. Good food darling. Buena comida.

I'm allowed, he would say to me and my brother.

I had seen my father touch the ladies. I had seen him touch their asses.

My father's coffee was blacker than theirs, made in his own pot. The ladies spooned him sugar.

Some ladies wore masks after eating their pan de agua. The factory air was dusty.

Once I said, Funny.

My father said, What.

Dust, I said. Here.

He said, You don't know funny.

* * *

In Baltimore was the park on the hill where under the sand was wet.

China, I said, if you dig deep enough.

My brother's sneakers never looked right.

There were days I could barely look at him.

In the park were monkey bars. Rusted swing sets.

There was a slide where we slid into sand.

My brother and I went to the park after school. The monkey bars at the park were higher than the ones in the schoolyard. We perched on the monkey bars and watched the sunset. The sky turned orange. Then back to blue. We could see the whole city lit up below. We never talked. We sometimes heard gunshots. We mostly listened to traffic.

There was a time my father would say to me, One day it's yours.

All of it, he would say.

He would gesture to what. A hotel room. A factory. A view. The leather inside of a rented car.

And I would say, I don't want it.

And he would say, You don't know what you want.

And I would say, I know what I don't want.

And he would say, You don't know shit.

And my brother would put his headphones on and turn up the metal and rock his head in a retard way.

And my father would look at me.

And the feeling in my gut.

When my father called England and France he waved us away and mouthed, England, or, France. He said, Go.

Outside goats ate the parking lot weeds. My brother and I threw sticks to the goats. They were so stupid these island goats. Sometimes they ate the sticks. And sometimes they came running at us like dogs.

The ladies' husbands pulled into the lot. They waited in their cars in cotton shirts. They smoked cigarettes down to the filters and flicked their filters to the lot. All of the goats would go after the filters. The husbands never laughed at the goats. Their windows were open even in rain. Fast-speed island music played. When the husbands waved we looked at the ground.

* * *

On the low-lit street the date ran off.

Sure she ran, my father said. She was scared, he said. She's young.

He wore a ski cap, he said. Imagine. A coat.

On an island for God's sake, said my father.

He said, Who wears a coat on an island.

Then pow, said my father.

Sure she ran.

Brass knuckles, he said.

Lousy island, he said.

He pulled my nose.

Eat your eggs, he said.

Maryland. Shaped like a gun. The city not far from the trigger. A house in the city. A bedroom in the house. A bed in the bedroom pushed to the wall. Under the blanket. Morning in winter. A streak of light piercing the curtain. Dust forming in the streak of light. A single dot of dust. Its flight across the room.

On a ride in the sports car, it was me and my father's date in the back.

The best-looking one in the factory, he said. Boy look at that body. Out to here.

Look at her body boy, said my father. You won't see that in the States.

My brother sat in the front. He read a comic and listened through headphones.

The spitting image, said my father slapping his back. A son of a gun.

This was a Friday. He drove us to a dinner in the city. We took the highway. We were speeding to get there. The lady drivers were the worst, said my father. The ladies shouldn't even have a license, he said. Watch this, he said as he cut one off. Watch this.

They swore in Spanish at my father.

He said, That'll show them to mess with a genius.

* * *

A man in San Juan grabbed my father's shirt. He punched my father's face. My father fell.

So this was my father lying in the street. My father with a bloody nose. Blood on his best cotton shirt. My rich white American father, an inventor of something that let people breathe.

This wasn't your father.

I wish it had been yours.

Then I could say the right things to you and we could have a drink and maybe laugh at the thought of your father all fucked-up in the street.

But your father would never have been lying on some low-lit street in San Juan.

Your father would never have been bleeding like that, like some stupid fucker, just bleeding like that.

I asked my father about the dust.

I said, Where does it go.

He said, It goes in the filter.

It gets crushed, he said.

Then what, I said.

He said, It stays in the filter.

But what if it gets out, I said.

He said, It won't get out.

I said, But what if rats in the landfills chew through the filters.

He said, Rats cannot chew through the filters.

I said, Yes they can.

He said, No they can't.

I said, Yes they can.

He said, Do you want to be poor.

There was a day my brother and I were looking through my father's failed inventions for no good reason other than my mother would die and she wanted the house clean, and we were cleaning the room where he kept his failed inventions, his assembled bits of wire and foam and string and metal, and we laughed pretty hard when my brother picked up some crazy-looking object, an object that looked like a robot built by retard kids, and I remember saying, What the fuck, and my brother said, Look, and put the object on a table and pushed a small red button on its front, and the whole thing shook then split in two.

When my brother and I perched on the monkey bars no one could see us. It was too dark. And we were too high up. Not even the kids who stood below us could see us up there.

The kids were drunk. Sometimes they threw bottles at each other. Sometimes we got sprayed from the crashing bottles.

Sometimes the kids pissed into the sand. They were crazy kids. Girls and boys. And they couldn't see us where we perched.

It was hard not to laugh. We knew we could have scared them. We knew we could have jumped onto their backs. It scared us to think how we could scare them. We could have made them piss their pants.

But we liked the park.

So we held our breath.

We sat, silent, unmoving.

Some masks didn't work. These came back to the island in dirty boxes. Some of the boxes were very small and crammed with masks. The boxes were piled in the factory.

My father would blame the ladies.

You're not sewing them tight, he would say.

Peru would call. And Mexico.

Those days my father slammed his fist to the desk.

He stared at the pile of boxes.

He screamed for hours into the phone.

He would say, You're just not using them right.

Those days my brother watched the ladies work. I sat in the lot with the goats. I waited for the husbands to wait for the ladies.

Mornings in Baltimore. Winter mornings. The curtain pierced by a streak of light. And dust rode on the streak of light. And if I waved my pillow the dust would scatter. I would choose a single dot of dust. It would travel

upward like a leaf in a storm. Like a single snowflake in a gust of air. It would pass forever through space and time. This speck of ancient human skin. The air was always full of dust. And nothing could crush it.

On the ride to our dinner in the city my father said, Listen.

He talked of factories in foreign countries.

You don't want to know, he said.

But he at least made a filter to help.

He looked at me in the rearview mirror.

Sweatshops, he said. Now they can breathe.

He said, That's my job.

I looked out at the wilted highway palms.

He said, Listen.

In the rearview mirror he was eyes and eyebrows. A piece of forehead.

He said, There's dangerous dust all around us.

He said, My filter can crush the dust.

It's a killer, he said pointing his hand like a gun at my brother's head.

The date picked dirt out from under her nails. Her nails were red and very long.

He said, Do me a favor.

He said, Please don't talk.

I'm not talking, I said.

He said, Shut your face.

He said, Don't even start.

Other drivers looked at us. Some were men. Their windows were open, their arms out the windows. Our windows were up.

My father said, What do you know about landfills.

But I wasn't thinking about the rats. About their sharp teeth chewing straight through the filters. The dangerous dust released.

I was watching a kid in the car next to ours. He was in the back seat like I was. He was watching me through the window too, but then he was gone.

My brother said nothing, reading his comic. We could hear his music.

My father said, What does she know. He looked at my brother. He said, Your sister's crazy. He laughed. He nudged my brother's arm.

My brother was off in his own crazy world. Who knew what he

thought. His brain was made of dirt. Or shells. Or rotten fruit.

My father's forehead was sweating. The back of his neck was sweating. He said, You don't know shit. He smacked the wheel. He said, You just don't know.

There was dried grass all along the roadside. Signs for things. Drinks. Chickens, live and cooked.

He smacked the wheel. He said, What do you know.

Empanadas. Succulent ribs. Lemon-lime drink.

You know nothing, he said.

Homestyle empanadas. Like your mother's empanadas.

My mother made no empanadas.

We had regular food. American food.

Fried chicken in a bucket. Buttered rolls in a bucket. Regular drinks.

He said, Listen to me.

He said, You don't listen.

Then he slowly stopped the car in a lane on the highway. The date said something sad in Spanish. Cars screeched to a stop behind us. My father put the car into park. He got out of the car and walked into traffic.

In California my father rented a car and took us to theme parks. My brother and I rode the rides while my father sat on a bench drinking coffee from a paper cup.

At one park we could pan for gold. We left the park with vials of dirt. There were specks of gold in the dirt. It was hard to see the specks.

Hold that dirt, said my father.

You'll be rich, he said.

He took us to a restaurant, and the city blinked below us.

The wine made me feel like I could laugh. My brother's face was red.

My father said, This is the life.

I said, What do you mean.

I mean the life, he said.

Big deal, I said. And I knew that if I laughed my brother would start laughing too. And I knew that if my brother started that every person in the restaurant would turn and stare because my brother sounded like a retard, and now he was drunk, as well.

So I held my breath and thought of my mother dying.

* * *

There was a time my father would say to me, One day it's yours.

I would take over. The men would work for me. The ladies too.

But the rats, I would say.

So my brother could take over instead. My brother the genius who couldn't tie a shoe.

The kids who came to the park at night were drunk. They were the wild kind of kids. They threw bottles and hard. They were looking for a fight. They could have killed us you know.

I imagine your father lying there on that street and how I would think what a fuckup, your father, and I would tell you this, and maybe we would laugh together over a drink and I would confess to you that my father, too, was a fuckup.

But it was my father lying in the street like that, and so I'm kind of alone here, you see, because your father, though maybe a fuckup in his own fucked-up way, is not the fuckup mine is.

Your father would never have been there, and you know it, and we will never have a drink and laugh it up.

We were sitting the three of us in a lane on the highway. On a Friday of all days. Car horns blaring. Cars swerving around us. It was me and the date in the backseat. My brother's music went all the way up. My father was walking along the shoulder. Then he shrunk out of sight. A goat was walking along the shoulder. My brother saw the goat and laughed. Cars were nearly hitting us. I don't have to tell you how fast they were going. Our car shook when the others passed. It occurred to me to drive the car. But I didn't know how to drive yet. My father's date was crying. I wasn't old enough to drive. I said to the date, Drive the car. I wasn't nice in how I said it. Her shoulders were shaking. She looked so stupid. Like a stupid kid. Her shoulders shook from crying. I said, Drive-o the fucking car-o. I pointed to the steering wheel. I made my hands like I was driving. I yanked on her arm.

I screamed, Drive-o drive-o. She climbed over into the driver's seat. I looked at her ass when she climbed over. Her pants were tight and pink. My brother moved his head to his music. He laughed but he couldn't hear himself laugh. He couldn't hear how stupid he sounded, how fucking retarded, and I can't even tell you what it did to me when he laughed like this. What it did to me in my gut. I said, Stop it you retard. Stop it you retard fucker. Look, he couldn't hear me. And he wasn't retarded. He was wired wrong. And we were about to be killed and it wasn't by our own choosing. The date drove slow and found my father walking. The goat was walking with him. Minutes we crept beside the two. My father walking rigid. His face and neck were red. The goat bounced beside him. The cars behind us nearly slammed us. I screamed at my brother to roll down his window. I took his headphones off his ears. I screamed again. Then my brother was crying. I screamed at my father to get in the car. I said to the date, Stop that crying el stupid-o bitch-o. The cars behind us nearly killed us. The goat ran into brown weeds off the highway.

I imagine my father laughs at some point, lying there on his back, facing nothing, the sky, and who knows what it looked like, the sky, that night, and, really, who cares.

I imagine, too, he had a bit too much to drink, and suddenly the whole thing seems very funny to my father, lying there, a fucking genius, an inventor for fuck's sake, his back pressed to the street.

Then he tries to move his arms to get himself up and the pain moves in faster than he can lift his body from the ground and he starts thinking it's not really so funny anymore, this life, the utter absurdity of it all, this life, I mean, really, the minute by minute tedious choice between pain and death.

Is this too much.

On the low-lit street the date ran like hell. She didn't come in to work the next morning.

She left me there, my father said.

My father and I sat at the table. No one was eating. My brother sat on the floor.

Pow, said my father.

Brass knuckles, he said.

And, he said, he has my wallet.

And he really socked me good.

My brother laughed.

My father looked over at my brother.

My father said, Is something funny.

My brother was laughing on the floor.

My father got up and walked toward my brother. My brother's sneakers were cockeyed, the Velcro undone.

My father was staring, noticing something.

I said, Don't stare.

He said, Tie your shoes, son.

But there were no ties.

He said, Did you hear me, son.

He walked closer to my brother.

My brother back-crept to a corner.

My father said, You think this is funny.

He said, You think it's funny that your father got socked.

My brother laughed. I knew he was laughing at the word socked. I knew he would think this word was funny. And my father said it thick and slurred. It sounded more like thocked. And that was funny.

My father said, What's funny, son.

I said, Did you thock him back.

My father turned to look at me. His eyelids were swollen.

Who do you think you are, he said.

You should have thocked him, I said.

My father's nose was bleeding again.

My brother was laughing his head off.

My father turned to my brother.

I picked up the pitcher.

You should have thocked him, I said.

My father turned. He said, You know nothing.

He said, Do yourself a favor. He said, Put that pitcher down.

You should have crushed him, I said.

I was standing by the table.

Then I was standing on a chair.

He said, Get off that chair.

My brother put his headphones on. He turned his music up. I could hear his music. Some metal song I had heard before. And I heard the ocean. Or was it the air. Something whistled. My brother's head rocked. Light came from the window. There were millions of dust specks in the light. I said, This place is fucking dusty. I laughed at this. My father did not. He lifted his plate. He raised it higher. I threw the pitcher. He threw the plate.

As my father was getting back into the car he said to me, You don't know shit.

The date climbed into the back.

Drivers swore at us. My father drove. We ate somewhere in the city. Rice and beans. Plantains. Everything was soft and wet.

My brother read his comic. He wore his headphones.

The date looked at her lap. She was devout. A good one. But her pants were pink and up her crack. In the States she would have been another kind of lady. My brother and I saw this kind of lady when we took the long way home from the park. Some of the ladies were men. They called my brother Sugar. This made my brother laugh.

I should say, before I forget, that I liked the city. San Juan. Music came from every doorway. There were dogs on the sidewalks. Hookers on the sidewalks. Smells like the smell of burning meat.

On the ride home from dinner no one spoke. I sat as far from the date as I could. I pressed my face to the window and thought of my face pressed to the window. I thought of what it looked like from the other side. I thought of some kid in another backseat. How he would look at me with my face pressed tight. He would know I was stupid and from the States. He would know I couldn't climb a palm. I couldn't split a coconut. I liked American coconut shredded in a bag. Hamburgers on rolls. Kentucky Fried. And I thought of the goat who ran into weeds. And I thought of how to find the goat. And if I found the goat of what I would do. I would treat it like it was a dog.

*   *   *

I don't believe there was a man in a ski cap. I think the date punched my father in the face. I think the date's husband punched my father in the face. I think a hooker punched my father in the face. I think a wild kid stabbed my father in the face. I think a lady driver ran over my father's face. I think a Coco Loco split open my father's face. I think the concierge shot my father in the face. I think the goats bit my father's face. I think the rats chewed my father's face. I think the ghost of my mother punched my father in the face. I think my brother laughed in my father's face. I think I threw a pitcher at my father's face. I threw a pitcher at my father's face. I was aiming for my father's face. My father ducked. I threw a pitcher at the wall behind my father.

My brother was the one called retarded in school, and I was the one to punch the kids who called him retarded.

And my brother could say the alphabet backward and he could count backward and he could do other things that I couldn't do.

And I wasn't retarded.

There was a night, late, my father out, my brother and I sneaked to the beach. We saw kids on the beach and a fire burning. The Coco Locos and their friends around a fire.

When they saw us they screamed out, America.

They said, Stupid fucks.

But they laughed so we walked even closer.

A radio on the sand played fast-speed music. Some kids danced in the sand by the fire. Sparks from the fire scared my brother. He looked like he was about to cry. He started to back-creep to the hotel. I felt that weirdness in my gut. But before I could call him a fucking retard, and before someone else could call him a retard, and before I could punch that person in the face, someone, a girl, held my brother's arm. Next thing my brother was walking toward the fire. Next he was dancing on the sand. I have to say he danced like a retard. It wasn't his kind of music.

And there was a night my brother and I walked home from the city park.

The street was unlit and we were the only ones. A car slowed beside us. We kept on walking. It was Baltimore and we knew how to get home. The car crept along and we walked a bit faster. The window went down. The man said, Get in, and we ran.

And I always wondered, years after the man slowed his car and said, Get in, where we might have gone had we gotten in.

There was bread on the floor. Fruit on the floor. Splinters of glass and broken dishes. Egg yolk stuck to the walls. To my arms.

I was still standing on the chair.

The silver pitcher had rolled back and back and back then stopped.

My brother went to the factory. The ladies would give him pan de agua. They would call him Sweetie and play with his hair.

I don't know how long we stood like that.

My father picked up the pitcher.

I don't need to say how fucked-up it was.

My father said, Who do you think you are.

I was taller on the chair. I was crazy, monstrous, on the chair.

I said, Who do you think you are.

The pitcher had hit the wall behind him. It was all fucked-up. I don't need to say how dented.

My father said, I know who I am.

I wanted to see myself on the pitcher. It was all dented now. I wanted to see what the pitcher could do.

My father said, You know who I am.

I could have jumped him from the chair. I could have made him piss his pants.

I'm a genius, he said.

I could have crushed him to bits.

I'm your father, he said.

My brother could hang upside-down on the monkey bars and the blood never rushed to his head.

He could jump off the monkey bars and land on his knees or his face or his back and not cry.

So he was the one to jump off the monkey bars that one time, that last time we went to the park. He was the one to land on those kids and I was the one laughing my ass off.

And on the monkey bars that last time, I remember thinking, Don't do it, because I could feel what he was about to do.

And I remember thinking, Do it already, because who knows why. I just did.

My mother had already died. My father was moving around the house. He was putting things into boxes and bags. He was trashing his failed inventions. None worked the way they should have worked. We were leaving for the summer for the island.

So that one time, the last time we went to the park, my brother jumped onto those kids.

And I can't tell you how scared those kids were. I mean they nearly died. They never saw it coming. I just laughed my ass off. And at that moment I felt very alive. And I knew that I was very alive. And I knew that the moment would pass. And that's how I knew I was very alive and that living was the step before not living. I mean that living was the step before dust. And dust was some crazy kind of eternal. And the whole world felt crazy, and I was laughing too hard. And before I fell from laughing so hard I was yanked down from my perch. And we both got punched and punched and punched. And it was worth it.

But every time before that time we sat there silent, unmoving.

At home my mother drifted in and out of what was next.

My father, the TV blue on his face, half-slept on the edge of a chair.

Below the kids pissed onto the swings.

The kids made out in the sand.

The city blinked like stars.

And when the sky was blackest and the kids left the park, my brother and I jumped down from our perch and walked the long way home.

STATEMENT OF PURPOSE

by KEVIN MOFFETT

THE TWO OF THEM, Ben and Adria, meeting in a manatee pool. The pool, part of Manatee Encounter, is edged by smooth-topped coquina rocks on which elderly couples sun themselves, apparently tired of communing with the lumbering sea life. "Nature's speed bumps," one of the men says. The elderly couples watch the rehabilitated manatees swim around and around beneath Ben and Adria, the sole humans in the pool, who tread water in black life jackets. "Mauled by boats, all of them," one of the wives says.

Ben is waiting for the manatees to resurface. Below him he can see the animals' dim dun shapes, prehistorically slow. He has been considering trying to mount the big cow they call Michelle, but he figures the handlers would have a way of humiliating him publicly if he did. He thinks, Men throughout history have discovered animals and ridden them. "If I could rig up a water-safe harness," he says aloud. "A proper saddle, I mean."

"What then?" Adria says.

He turns his attention to this woman with orangish water-slicked-back hair. Her face is thin and sunburned and plain. "The earliest explorers mistook manatees for mermaids," she says. "Ever since, there's been sort of a love/hate thing with the manatee."

She smiles, becomes embarrassed, smiles wider. Her top teeth are crooked, a trait Ben finds instantly, unequivocally sexy. The teeth make him want to make her laugh. "What I think the manatee needs to do is make itself available to be ridden," he says. "America loves an animal it can ride. You think anyone's going to *eat* a horse, or plow through a herd of them in a Chris-Craft? People have incredibly complex feelings for the horse."

She laughs. Treading water in front of her, he thinks of bad girls gone schoolgirl, schoolgirls gone bad. The water is warm, which is how the manatees, down below them, bothering the water with their slowness, like it.

Ben likes propositions of all kinds, including ones he knows he'll never act on, *especially* ones he knows he'll never act on. He is a man with a high tolerance for possibility. His life jacket, too small for him, makes him look like a well-meaning impostor. His Adam's apple bobs above and below the water's surface. A manatee appears close behind Adria, sneezes out a spray of water, and he gets a warm and uncomplicated feeling. He says, "Here's the part where I ask a question and you promise not to be spooked off."

She promises without pause. He thinks of the best way to construct what he wants to ask, so the surprise of the request will overshadow most possible menace. The important thing in a situation like this is to phrase the request as nonchalantly, as delicately as possible. He says, "Can I ride you?"

Ben calling ten minutes after dropping her off at her house. They've been to see a movie about a group of veterans in wheelchairs who solve murders. Ben's voice sounds huskier, more determined than earlier. "I need to know something," he says. "Don't think I'm crazy."

Before Adria has a chance to answer, he says, "Will you stick around if I get paralyzed?"

Adria has the brief suspicion this isn't Ben on the telephone but somebody else. She says, "Of course I will."

"Paraplegia, I mean, waist-down. I'm in a wheelchair but can change my clothes and shave, comb my hair. You won't need to do any of that. Digestive function: normal. Sexual function: normal. Listen, from the get-go I'm determined not to let my affliction slow me down. I'm active in wheelchair sports, advocacy groups, select political campaigns. Soon we're going to forget all about this."

"I'm not going anywhere."

Ben says, "I'll definitely be putting a mini license plate on the back of the wheelchair. Something uplifting. For the kids."

She is afraid to tell her friends about Ben. They'll ask questions she doesn't know the answers to. Marta and Sarah, Melissa, Amanda, Jennifer, Rachel, and Steph. Adria's friends are pretty and she is not. They meet men who work in marketing, men who enjoy specific, tangible things, like cunnilingus and microbrewed beer. Ben has never really talked about what he does for a living.

"If I lost function in my arms I could mouth-paint," he says.

She likes him past any conceivable explanation of why she likes him. She wakes up in the morning with a head full of plans. She wants to relearn the trumpet, relearn Spanish. She's been thinking about having herself refitted for braces.

"I *know* I'd do something exceptional," he says.

She has known him two weeks.

Ben and his policy of giving a woman a coffee mug, handing it to her, unwrapped, at the end of the eighth date and carefully monitoring her response. The way a woman reacts when handed an unwrapped coffee mug tells him much of what he needs to know about her. An overly favorable reaction toward the mug is not ideal. It shows a false congeniality, a graciousness out of proportion to the gift, because what kind of gift is a coffee mug? When the congeniality is exhausted, where will they be then? A negative reaction to the mug, this is closer to adequate. Yes, simple honesty is what Ben is looking for. Or, failing that, dishonest restraint rendered plausibly. Actually, Ben isn't sure what he is looking for.

In Adria's car, parked in front of Ben's apartment, he talks about the Tampa Bay Buccaneers. He has been a loyal fan of the team since 1976, the year they went 0–14, and now that they have changed stadiums and uniforms and have won the Super Bowl, he finds himself discontented. "I could *understand* them when they were losers," he says. "Now, even the players' names, *Griese, Pittman, Alstott,* they sound like action movies, like dudes in action movies. The new coach works sixteen-hour days. A *football* coach working *sixteen-hour days…*" He trails off to let himself stew temporarily in the sweet betrayal of the Tampa Bay Buccaneers' success. This is one of his favorite things to do.

"You're a friend of the underdog," Adria says. "If you weren't, you would've never been out there swimming with the manatees. And we would've never met. It's a good—"

In the middle of her sentence, Ben reaches into his backpack and presents her with the mug. Adria, caught on the end of a word, appraises the mug noncommittally. Her eyes shift from it to Ben to it. "It's a good characteristic," she finishes.

Returning her attention to the mug she says, "I don't drink coffee."

"That's okay. It should work with other liquids."

"I'd been thinking about starting something new, I mean."

She stares at the mug and smiles. Lately Ben has begun forcing himself to look away from her teeth when she bares them, they're so alluring. The crooked teeth are an unfair advantage. What happened to him that he's now so moved by imperfection? Bad football teams, women with crooked teeth, with leg bruises, on crutches, women in wigs, very short women, women with poor posture, with lazy eyes, with neck braces, arm-slings, stretch marks, missing fingers, acne, rosacea, psoriasis, mangled toes, arm fat, women with skin grafts, burns, and other scars, scars, in particular those glorious raised red keloid scars.

When Adria is finished smiling, her bottom lip snags on her tooth. To Ben, turning back to her, this is just too damn much. He surrenders and kisses her, running his tongue along the jagged back gate of her teeth. He smells a soapy smell as Adria swallows deeply and holds her breath—she always does this when they kiss. It lends the kisses a solemn and metered aspect.

He did not monitor her reaction to the mug closely enough. Before he gets out of the car to go into his apartment, he looks at her one more time. Her nose is treaded with blackheads, football-textured. Her hair, tinted a pumpkin color, is too short; her eyes, too closely set. From a distance her irises blend with her pupils and are as black and inert as an umlaut.

She has him.

"Night," he says, reaching for the door handle.

"Ben," she says. She leans over, kisses him on the cheek, and pauses, staring at the mark her lipstick made. She says, "You're perfect."

He smiles. "...said the spider to the fly," he says.

*   *   *

Adria wondering, When is he going to ride me? There are many things about which she cannot think rationally. Sex is one of these things. She's had it on nine occasions, each time with a different stranger who groped her for a few minutes before tearing off her clothes and seesawing atop her, emitting low reptile grunts. A few of them called her *baby* as in *baby, yeah, that's right, baby, oh, you like how I'm deep-dogging you, baby?* and made her long for a scrap, however brief, of honest communion, like between parent and baby, not these sorry snakepit pump-ruts. By the third time, she found that if she remained absolutely still, the operation ended soon enough. The worst part, though, came next: postcoital conversation, during which Adria's fantasies swayed between the homicidal and the suicidal. A man who talks about his penis in the third person, referring to it as *he,* is, to Adria's mind, capable of any imaginable atrocity, and should be injured and banished. A man who knows how and when to shut up is a comrade for life, even if she thinks she'll never see him again. Especially if she thinks she'll never see him again.

Contrary to his proposal in the manatee pool, Ben has yet to make a discernible advance toward riding her. His tentativeness pleases her: it shows he is less unhinged than she previously supposed, that he is in possession of some gallant logic. His tentativeness also worries her: maybe he isn't interested in riding her. Maybe the proposal was strictly figurative, like the song "Give Me Your Heart." As a teenager, Adria answered a survey in a *Seventeen* magazine called "Is Your Boy a Cold-Timing Charlie?" with multiple-choice questions like "Does he use tongue when he's kissing you? If yes, how much tongue?"

In high school Adria's mother told her that she, Adria, was just going through some awkward years, that she would grow up to be beautiful when the acne cleared and she figured out how to apply makeup. Adria had been a striking baby, her mother assured her. People used to come up to baby Adria and say, "Now *that* is a handsome baby." Adria didn't care. Early on, she noticed how pretty girls bloomed and blanched from being stared at. It was the end of their internal life, beauty being its own kind of minor celebrity in the beach town where she grew up. Everything about these girls, women now, some of whom Adria has remained friends with, is turned outward. When she's with them, Adria watches men watch them. The men try to erase the women's advantage with a proprietary, predatory regard that Adria knows she could never shoulder. Her friends seem to ignore it away.

Why didn't Ben's proposition in the manatee pool seem sinister? Adria was going to answer, "Hop on," but before she could, one of the manatee handlers appeared atop the rocks and said, "Time's up, lovebirds." Writing his phone number on a Manatee Encounter cocktail napkin, Ben told her he liked the sound of it: *lovebirds.*

She learns things about him, slowly and almost always by accident. He'll let slip a tentative memory here, a preference or prejudice there. He likes watching nature shows on television. He is scared of wasps and bees. His father, retired in Arizona, used to work as a librarian, and Ben reads all the time. One of his favorite books is called *How We Die,* written in excruciatingly clear-eyed detail by a surgeon hoping to demystify and deromanticize death. The surgeon describes a time when he pulled the heart out of a cardiac-arresting man's chest with the intention of massaging the heart back to life, and instead watched it fibrillate and die in his hands. Ben reads a passage aloud to Adria, where the surgeon compares the fibrillating heart to a "wet, jellylike bagful of hyperactive worms."

The two of them are sitting face-to-face on a velour couch in Ben's living room. Their legs are interlocked and each time Ben pauses to carefully enunciate one of the more clinical terms—*thoracotomy, pericardium, ventricular*—Adria feels a jellylike hyperactivity in her own thorax. She listens and plays with the hair on his calves, trying to nat it into balls by rubbing it in little circles. Ben has such pristine leg fur, soft as lanugo. Adria rubs, rubs. What else is good about Ben? He has big red lips. His good humor is inscribed on his face. He is erratically irreverent. Much of the time he appears to be thinking aloud, trying to arrive at what he wants to say by saying it. He doesn't banter. He doesn't volley. He isn't trying to promote a public notion of his own intelligence.

He is kind to her. He likes her.

Ben reads, "At the time the fibrillating patient's life came to its abrupt end, the outcome of his heart's misbehavior was inescapable."

Behind him, a shaded standing lamp casts an almondy glow over the couch. Adria finds herself passing in and out of attentiveness, still rubbing and staring at Ben's leg hair. When is he going to ride her? His body is slim and unobtrusive. Often he smells like the beach. He probably looks excellent in formal wear, or at the bedside of a dying relative, or captaining a boat, or leaning on his elbow in front of a campfire, or holding a newborn baby, or tied naked to a La-Z-Boy. His toes are unbelievable.

"There are few reliable accounts," he reads, "of the ways in which we die."
His voice, his voice is like some vital jungle thing.
He will leave her. He is going to leave her.

Alone at home, Ben watching a TV show about manatees. "When Florida's first explorers encountered what we now call the manatee," the narrator intones, "they were drunk on orange-wine and rum. Some of them actually jumped into the water and went after the hulking animals."

A story too preposterous to be untrue, Ben thinks, though Adria never mentioned that the explorers were drunk. Ben is glad to know they were. He hopes the explorers stayed drunk among the mermaids, delaying for a while full awareness of the gentle but unlovely sea cow, the forfeiture of possibility...

Adria calling her friend Melissa, who teaches kindergarten and collects stuffed animals, to tell her that she's been to Dr. Lentz, an orthodontist. Melissa had braces a few years ago to correct a slight, slight underbite. She answers the phone, "Who dis?" Adria can tell she's in one of her jovial moods. After the preliminary niceties are out of the way, Melissa starts in with the lingo—the jovial moods are always accompanied by the lingo. It goes something like: "Aw snap. Peep this: you gots to *chill*."

"I can't remember if they hurt or not," Adria says. "Are they going to hurt?"

"Girl, nuh-uh, not a bit."

This is Melissa's way of joking with Adria and their other friends, when she's in a jovial mood. It is her only exceptional characteristic.

"Lentz creeps me out with that singing. And the other patients, all of us in the same room together."

"You a trip, girl. You a maiden voyage."

Those who endeavor to be funny and are not are a sorry membership. Adria is thinking again about Ben, who seldom fails to be funny when he is trying to. It confers him with an immediate dignity Melissa will never know. Adria can hear her breathing heavily on the other end of the line.

"We're all, like, so *totally* glad you're doing this," Melissa says, back to normal.

Adria hasn't told Ben about the braces. She wants to surprise him. What does Melissa mean by *we*? Adria feels hastily discussed by her friends, manhandled. She says, "We?"

Ben at the flea market, studying an Amish woman behind a booth that offers a selection of puppies for sale. A handwritten sign, hanging from the back of a minivan with Pennsylvania license plates, says *Amish Puppies are Better'n Mennonite Puppies, Ask Why.* Next to the woman a half-dozen or so Amish kids, maybe hers, are behind a metal cage, playing with puppies. The kids hold up the puppies to anyone who passes near the cage. They babble with natural salesmanship while the puppies squirm in their arms. The woman, wearily seated in a wooden folding chair, seems subordinated by their happiness. Ben is moved by her posture of defeat but doesn't think the interest is strictly sexual. Maybe it is. Restraint makes her cenotaphic, emptily tempting. She wears a formless frock, and her face, crowned by a simple lace bonnet, is as unexceptional as a bowl of butter.

What does he know about the Amish? He knows they build barns and make bell harnesses for those Clydesdales in beer commercials. And that they're required to leave the farm the year they turn sixteen, to cavort with other Amish teenagers in rented apartments with whiskey and satellite TV to see if they prefer it over the barn building and the bell-harness making. Ben thinks the Amish are fascinating and ridiculous. This woman, she's maybe twenty-five, thirty at the oldest, wasting the day away selling Amish puppies, wilting at night under the pious girth of some Jebediah or Ezekiel, who waits until she's fallen asleep to crawl over the two-by-four they've nailed down the middle of their homemade bed for modesty...

Ben forces himself to think about Adria.

Today he is trying to find a gift for her at the flea market. A real gift, one that he hopes will serve as a statement of purpose. Unlike the mug, which Adria has taken up coffee drinking to make use of, Ben intends this gift to err on the side of the dramatic. Ben is not going to leave Adria. He no longer thinks about leaving Adria.

When they are not together, Ben notices that the memory of her is slow to summon, but once it does, for the rest of the day he carries an image of her slanted loveliness around with him. She has recently tried to dye her hair back to its natural color, which is a kind of late-bruise brownish red, and she has begun to wear nail polish and outlandish jewelry, and Ben has a hard time pinning down the general effect. They've been together nearly four months and still he has not ridden her. They haven't discussed the not-riding; they haven't discussed the not-discussing-the-not-riding. They talk about... What is it Ben and Adria talk about? They talk about Adria's friends. They talk about the books they read. They talk about things they've done and things, with the exception of riding, they want to do. They talk about and about.

Ben envisions giving her the statement-of-purpose gift at his apartment, the two of them quietly agreeing on its appropriateness and generosity, and then him leading her into his bedroom for him to finally, alas, ride her. He pictures wrapping paper on the floor, a general frolicking. And later, Adria wrapped in one of his towels standing in a lighted doorway.

What is good about Adria? She is unselfishly sentimental. She is unafraid of silence or whether the stories she tells reflect poorly on her. She is far more respectful of others than they are of her. Her sincerity is contagious, unaffected, becoming. Her interest in clothing is minimal. Her crooked teeth have gone from a distinct alluring oddity to just another element of her face. She is no longer a novelty. To him, she is beautiful.

But what gift? What will say what Ben cannot?

Ben starts over to the booth. Up close, he notices that the children are exquisite. There are five of them, three girls, two boys, each identically wheat-faced and farm-radiant, like little collectible dolls. Standing outside the metal cage that houses them and the puppies, Ben is hesitant to talk to them, afraid he'll somehow corrupt them with his urgency.

One of the little girls notices him and hands him a puppy. It tenses when it lands in Ben's grip, briefly, then relaxes again. He holds it out in front of him with both hands like an offering. The puppy, some kind of husky or chow mixture, is cosmically soft and white with a black spot on its side, eyes tightly shut, quivering, barely past the point of being born. The puppy has been born, but it doesn't know it's been born. Its dream-mind has not yet surrendered from sleep. This, to Ben, is a wonderful, a near-religious, notion. He leans down and carefully rests his face in the dog's soft stomach fur.

"Why are Amish puppies better'n Mennonite puppies?" he asks the little girl.

The girl shrugs. She has picked up another puppy and is looking

around for somebody to unload it on. "Mommy, why are our puppies better?" she asks the woman in the folding wooden chair.

The woman, staring at her shoes, doesn't look up. "Tell the man those aren't the better puppies."

The Amish woman's teeth are crooked, Ben notices.

"She says these aren't the better puppies."

"I heard her," Ben says to the girl. "The man can hear you," he says to the woman, who's about ten feet away. The woman doesn't acknowledge him; she continues to imperially scowl at her scuffed black shoes. "I said I can hear you," he repeats, louder this time. And suddenly he hates this woman and her puritan apathy for souring his moment with the puppy.

Ben looks down again at the little animal sleeping in his hands. It has given itself to him totally. He thinks, Nobody needs to tell us we've been born. One day we just wake up. He asks the little girl, who has handed off the puppy and is reaching for another, "So how do you like being Amish so far?"

Back at his apartment, he calls Adria. "Look here, lovebird," he says. "How about coming over?" He has bought a dog leash, dog collar, dog bowls, dog bed, dog toys, dog food. The Amish puppy is asleep on the red tile floor by Ben's feet.

"I have an appointment," she says. "I'll come over after work tomorrow. I have a surprise for you."

"I like surprises," he says.

Adria beneath the wall-to-wall ceiling mirror in Dr. Lentz's office, six chairs arranged in a half-moon around a marble island of sinks. Adria, fully reclined, can see the chairs, the sink, Lentz, and the two assistants tightening wires and attaching rubber bands. Chair 1: boy with jet-black hair. Chair 2: boy in a hooded sweatshirt giggling at something, maybe her. Chair 3: Adria. Chair 4: girl with her mouth pried open, being worked on currently by Lentz and one of the assistants. From time to time the girl's eyes meet Adria's in the mirror. Chair 5: boy in wrestling sneakers having his wires tightened by the other assistant. Chair 6: very young girl who Adria overheard was having tiny spikes installed to correct a lisp.

Adria is waiting with a plastic harness in her mouth for her teeth to dry so Lentz can brush them with glue and apply brackets. Finished with the girl in Chair 4, he walks to the sinks and washes his hands. Adria is frightened of Dr. Lentz. He inspects the mouth of the boy with jet-black hair and says, "Rebrush!" and the boy gets up from the chair and sullenly walks over to a brushing station on the opposite side of the sinks, where an assistant shows him the proper way to brush. Lentz goes from chair to sink to chair, taking off and putting on disposable gloves, and crooning along with the rock muzak that plays from an unseen speaker. The orthodontist sings tough-faced, no joy in his delivery.

He and one of the assistants pull up stools next to Adria's chair. The assistant readies the pliers and glues while Lentz is singing "Choke me in the shallow water," a song Adria recognizes. Her mind measures the activity but doesn't analyze it. Lentz's hands, covered in white latex, are in her mouth. The assistant holds a curved tube firmly against the inside of Adria's cheek to suck saliva, probing around now and then to get at every drop. Lentz brushes the glue on and applies the brackets. His fingers delicately work their way around her teeth, attending to each of them. Watching in the mirror above as Lentz and his assistant lean over her, she feels scooped into, plumbed. "Do not swallow," the assistant says. The kids all look in the ceiling mirror, at her. The boy in the hooded sweatshirt is still giggling. Lentz sings, "I know what I know if you know what I mean." His hazel eyes, darting behind his thick-lensed glasses as he brushes the glue on and applies the brackets, suggest something panicking under ice.

Adria assures herself, They're fixing me. They're making me prettier.

"All set, you," Lentz says, patting the top of her thigh roughly. He's threaded the brackets with a wire, which is fixed into place with rubber bands. Adria runs her tongue along the outside of her teeth, top and bottom: little wire trestles from tooth to tooth.

As Dr. Lentz walks back to the island of sinks, the assistant says, "He's no prince, but he's a genius with teeth." She, too, pats Adria's thigh. "You should spit now, honey."

Adria with a bottle of wine, knocking on Ben's front door, her nod to propriety. Ben answers in a T-shirt and shorts. "Well, well, well," he says. She wears a red-and-white striped sundress and black cloth ballerina slippers. Her ankles are tan. Ben moves out of the doorway and makes an exaggerated welcome sweep with his arm, stopping her to kiss her before she walks by.

Something different about her hair, a new pair of turquoise earrings, eye shadow maybe. She sits down on his sofa, setting the wine bottle by her feet. Ben leaves the door open and walks over to the sofa. Adria is trying not to smile, trying not to smile. She smiles. Metal shine of brackets and wires, she looks at him with a hopeful but wounded expression. "Surprise," she says. She has to snap her lips forward to get them back over the braces.

Ben sits next to her on the sofa. He wipes his hands on his shorts, says, "Open back up," trying to sound genial, but it comes out irritable. He feels himself getting impatient. "Let's see what you, uh, got in there," trying genial, sounding irritable.

She smiles again, opens her mouth. Ben leans closer. Reaching into her mouth, he runs his finger slowly along the jagged brackets, a quarter-inch thick, working right now to correct her smile. He wants to hurry up and reach a consensus about them but all he can summon is a knee-jerk dislike toward the change. He liked her crooked teeth, he was *used* to her crooked teeth. Now it's the braces; after that, it will be the effect of the braces. In high school he was fond of several girls with braces. He thinks of them now: Jenny Ware, Missy Thompson, Darla Edinger. When the braces came off, their teeth looked like piano keys, long and straight. Adria is waiting for him to speak.

"Well, they're something," he says.

She snaps her lips forward, covering the braces.

"So, why now?" he says.

"I've been wanting to get them for a while. I don't know. I thought it seemed like a good time." The braces make her voice sound thin and nasally. More change. "You don't like them."

She shrugs and sighs. Her hesitancy, familiar to Ben, settles him down a little, although he still can't come up with anything judicious to say about the braces. Why don't his biases bear scrutiny? He should love the braces. He stands up and says, "Follow me."

Ben leading Adria by the hand into his bedroom, kicking a yellow squeaky toy out of the way. Adria tries to not anticipate disappointment. Ben tries to soften his impatience. Adria takes off Ben's shirt. Ben takes off Adria's dress. A gentle undoing. Adria's hands, Ben's voice. Slowness, Ben opens and closes his eyes, quickness, mutual regard, sweat, silence, silence. Aloneness. Dissolving

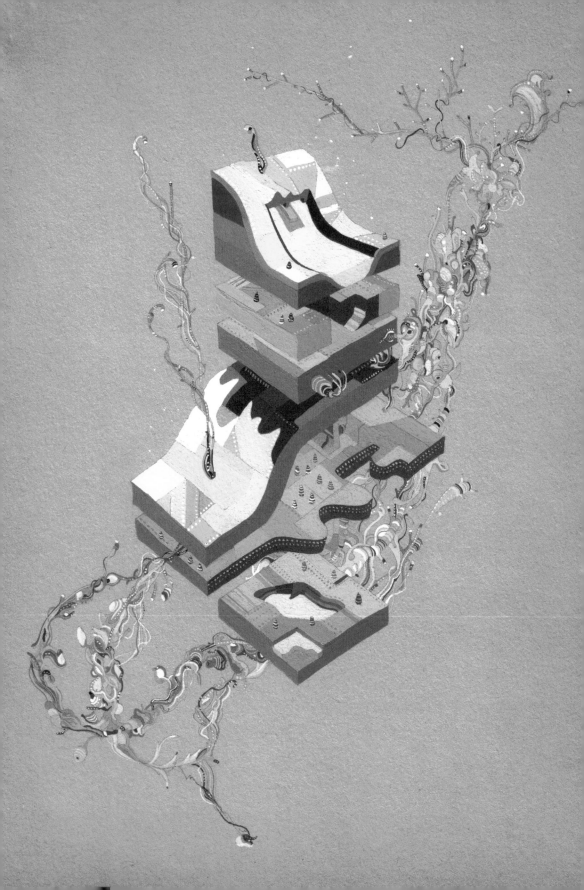

daylight. Glow-in-the-dark stars and planets on Ben's ceiling, like a little boy's room. Adria thinks about her friends again, rubbing Ben's chest hair in little circles, allowing herself a single comment. "That was a nice surprise." The sound of sprinklers, cicadas. Ben thinks: the puppy.

Ben scrambling out of bed, searching the floor for his clothes. Adria had been half-dreaming, half-wondering how she would describe this evening to her friends. The glow-in-the-dark stars, the sprinklers. Ben is leaving the room. First comes the shift, then the awareness of the shift. She feels lost already. She feels like calling out "Freeze" and stopping things. Ben returns.

"I put it in the bathroom," he says. "I was going to tell you to close your eyes and then I'd bring it out to you. It's gone. I forgot to shut the front door."

He sits with his back to her on the foot of the bed and tells her about the puppy, where he found it, his idea about it not yet knowing it's been born. Adria is having a hard time following him. She tries to sense where the evening is heading, wants to meet it before it gets there. Leaning over the edge of the bed, she finds her bra and struggles to put it on beneath the covers. "Let's find it," she says. "What's its name?"

"I haven't given it a name."

"What's it look like?"

"It's black with a white spot. It's cute and small, I don't know, it's Amish." His voice cracks on the last word.

The two get dressed and go outside to search for the puppy. The apartment is surrounded by chinaberry shrubs that Ben gets on his hands and knees to search under. Another starless night, the dumb glow of a full moon all over the sky. Adria calls, "Come on, puppy, puppy, puppy." She looks down at her dress and sees that she's put it on inside-out. The roots of her teeth are starting to hurt. "Puppy, puppy, puppy," she says. She wants to give the dog a name, but thinks that might somehow doom it. Watching Ben scramble around beneath the bushes, she tries to stem the pain by holding her hand to her mouth.

After another half-hour of searching the two go back inside the apartment. Adria sits down on the sofa, the bottle of wine still on the red tile floor in front of her, unopened. She had planned to say "Surprise" and then smile, not the other way around. First comes expectation, then disappointment. She closes her eyes. Her teeth are really hurting her now, a lively pain. She can feel each tooth tugged, and tugging back, the straight ones helping to align the crooked ones, tugging them down and allowing them to slip into place. It has always been this way. She was a striking baby, her mother used to say. In a few years men are gonna be chasing after you, just you wait. She waited. Her friends still call men *boys,* call successful dates *sleepovers.* The crooked ones tug and tug but the straight ones are tugging harder. Just you wait. She waited for years and then one came.

Ben turns the stereo on and sits down. Adria feels his sweaty arm come to rest around her shoulders, holding her next to him. He is breathing damply and heavily. Each breath seems to pull her a little closer to him, under him. "Well, well," he says. "Look what we have here."

Adria opens her eyes and looks at Ben, who is pointing to the corner of the living room.

The puppy. Sitting up in its purple bed in the corner, trying to lick itself awake. Yawning and shivering and opening its eyes. Ben says, "It was here all this time." Lifting his arm from her, he moves toward the puppy. He picks it up. "You nearly fooled us."

Adria nodding. Adria giving it a name.

CITY WATER

by BEN JAHN

SPRING CAME AND Pop sold half the flock and took his preaching on the road. As per usual, I set about to fuck up all gainfulness toward a future. Like Pop said on his radio sermon: a man is full of water; water runs downhill, seeks out the lowest places. One transgression feeds into another like runnel into river, until you're drifting in a fog-locked ocean of iniquity.

Off the air, he said this: "There's a luck shortage around here. Don't get what's in your head confused with good sense." He fingered the kennel latch. He could have been talking to the dogs, three boys kept from their bitch sister till she cooled. There was a low, gray ceiling on the sky—no hope for a blueing up with high whites and wind.

"I might be gone a good long while, you sell these dogs before they starve."

"Will do."

"Keep what you make on the wool," he said. But the price had dropped like a nickel in a well shaft. Last year's clip sat in twelve-foot gunnies in a ramshackle extension of the shearing shed. We both knew I couldn't give it away.

Well, there was no future. The land swaled down to Highway 101, a

flat rich piece of pasture that disappeared in a series of low dunes. Across the highway was marsh and slough, and white mounds of gravel dumped by the Eel. Beyond these the ocean cambered up to meet the sky. When I sold the fence line to the ad company, the huckster said: "You hate to see a billboard wreck a view like that." But I forged ahead, so to speak—leaving "Jr." off the dotted line. By the time he preached his way back, swindling youth groups and conning the brethren, I figured the ad money would change hands time and again.

I put another iron in the fire—I answered this ad in the biweekly: ARTIST NEEDS BARN. A guy named Dave Hawley, a burl-cutter out of Ferndale, had a commission to carve the state seal. One morning his red-wood block came up the lane on a log truck. It was a twenty-foot chunk of old growth, marbled heartwood, a thing to behold in itself.

I let him get settled in before we talked about rent. He built a scaffold, brought in a generator, strung lights in the rafters, and stocked a hardside cooler with Coors. When I came up, all he'd done was round off the corners and rough in the picture with black paint. "Minerva," said Hawley. "The old bitch. I should've done was bring a picture slide instead of freehanding it. But then accuracy ain't always a good thing."

We stood outside the barn, watched the dogs nip the flock into a rolling blanket, run them down along the fence toward the highway. I let my eyes drift to the main house, where Steph stood in the window staring down at whatever it was she saw in that dishwater.

"You want a piece of my commission, is that right?"

"I wouldn't," I said. I felt uneasy, knowing the barn would've gone unused. "I owe a friend."

"You going to shear those?"

"Carpet wool," I said. "Moth meal."

"You know who else pays rent," Hawley said. "Cartel."

"I thought about that. I seen their windshields bouncing sun off the ridge."

I headed out across the mudflats on the bankment highway, going toward Bill Scobie's—the bleakest stretch in Humboldt County. The barrack bank shuttered up with deal ply, the hobo tarps and lean-tos along the frontage, all gave off a damp, cold draftiness that took hold of me in a bad way.

I clamped the baffle against brackish air and tuned around on the AM band, skipping the gospel channels. President Reagan was somewhere doing something. Drugs. Drugs were everywhere. Drugs were running the world.

Scobie lived in a half prefab on a shifty spit of fill, a dry hump with tidal seepage each way you turned. I said half prefab. Half's my fault. I mean I didn't want to be a trucker. Just one of those things I talked about with a kid in the oven. One of those things like circling odd jobs in the help-wanteds. I helped truck Bill's house up from Healdsburg. All I remember is black ice and the guard rail, a sound like God's crowbar prying the gates of hell. Scobie's prefab washed into a defile south of Leggett, where the Eel snakes around Squaw Rock.

I could see Bill's wife Marlene in the yellow kitchen, her shape blurred by the milky plastic. They were living with the Visquine until I paid up.

Marlene opened the door and played her hip against the jamb. I noticed she wore a pair of Bill's jeans folded down twice at the waist, with a flannel, also Bill's, knotted to show her midriff.

"Homewrecker," she said. She had a swish-ass way of leading me back into the kitchen. The beauty queen in chew-can jeans, Miss Del Norte County, '84. She said, "Billboard's going up."

"Bones of it anyway." A crew had come and driven piles, built the frame.

"Why not pave it and start a drive-in movie?" She sat up on the drainboard. Behind her, out the window, the fog pulled apart along the cliffs, opening the view.

"Triple-X would pay you off in two weeks."

"I never said it."

"You were going to." I produced a soft pack and offered her a cigarette with the two rolled hundreds.

"I can't," she said, taking the money. "I'll get those lines on my lip, look like a mustache." She reached into a coffee can and brought up a fistful of grounds. "We bought a Mr. Coffee at the mall."

"We haven't gone down that way, since it opened—me or Steph."

"They have these live mannequins, real people, standing there straight-faced with sweaters tied around their shoulders."

"Real people."

"You never saw anything like it. Up on little platforms, roped off like they're worth extra for standing still and looking pretty." She filled the glass pot from the tap.

"Like I said, I haven't gone that direction."

"Maybe I'll just have a drag of yours," she said.

"He'll smell it on you. My brand, too."

"I'm gonna smoke a joint."

"Where's Bill?" I said.

Marlene turned and leaned over the sink to crank the window. "Out with Kater Murchison—*Ima pay the water bill, Marlene*—gone two hours. We're on city water now." She fired the joint, stayed twisted across the sink, gazing up the coast where the sun broached fog layers, tearing gaps to brighter space.

I thought of Steph, how the scoliosis forced her into the water, how the breech threw a wrench in all of it. After the baby, she lost the joint oil in her hips, all semblance of her gush-flow. Now she couldn't stand with intent a half hour at a time. I'd been sleeping on the porch since it happened, spitting on my dick for a year, going about my own business.

"Certain parts of Bill just aren't up to task," Marlene was saying. Coffee sputtered in the glass, started in smelling good.

"I don't believe that."

"You don't want to."

"Bill's an athlete," I said.

"Was."

"Don't be a cocktease."

"Why not?"

"You and Bill."

"Me and Bill fight eight nights a week—*Night shift calls you tell em I'm sick*—they'll think you tied one on—*tell em I tied one on, then*." The Mr. Coffee clicked off and she looked at it like she had no recollection of making it, no idea how it came to be on her counter. "Besides, I wouldn't tease if I thought you could handle serious."

Bill's truck geared down at the corner, pulled in next to mine in the sandy yard.

"Watch him feel your hood," Marlene said.

"You blame him?"

Bill had on his old HSU track sweatsuit, brittle shoulder-length blond hair, and black horn-rim glasses.

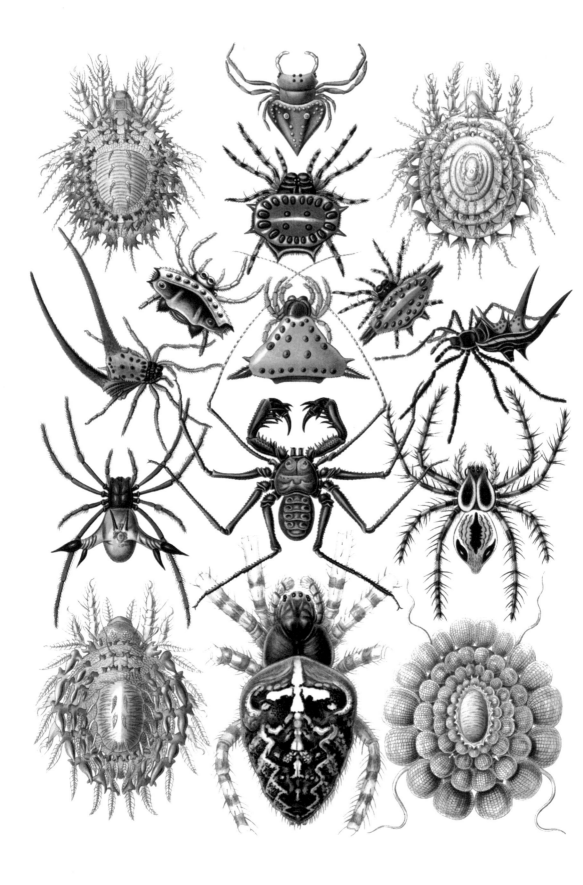

"Hey, Doyle."

"Bill."

"I had an idea."

"What is it, Bill?"

Bill sniffed the air. "You been smoking reefer again," he said. "Tried to lay the Folgers over it."

"I was showing Homewrecker the Mr. Coffee."

"That billboard went up in your south pasture, it's blank, right?"

"I've only seen the back of it, lately," I said.

"Kater and me and a couple other guys from the team, we got some old race footage. Thought we might stoke a fire and project onto the sign."

"Hills Brothers," Marlene said. "You said Folgers."

"Might work," I said. "Dave Hawley's got a Perkins gas generator."

"How's the seal coming?"

"He's roughing it in."

"I want to see it," Bill said.

"Homewrecker's Drive-In, come one, come all." Marlene said. "You know Bill never lost a race?"

"Everybody knows it," I said.

"He's like those mannequins, he ought to be on a pedestal—"

"I see where you're headed, Marlene. Marlene wants me to get a job at Sears."

"*I can't go from the mill to the mall, Marlene.*"

"Work is what I need," Bill said.

"That's what I said, Bill."

"You said job."

"You can bank on a job."

"Even if hauling greenchain at the mill was a job, I wouldn't call it that. It's a shift. I make a decision and time rolls along and that's a shift. Everything I do is a shift."

"You can bank on a job."

"The minute you start banking, things get shitted up."

"Speaking of shitted up," Marlene said, tasting the coffee. "I screwed the works. I forgot the filter."

"That's all right," I said. "I didn't want any."

*   *   *

I'd seen the cartel windshields above Tanner Creek. I drove the ridge road, overlooking the water, the tankers gleaming, and the white fogbank piling up past the bay's mouth. Hawley in the seat next to me, said: "Right now it's minus tides. You can see them out there with their davits dropped along the jetty. The Indians used to work the jacksmelt runs with surf nets, where they built the mall."

The ridge road topped out and threaded the broken chine, giving onto steep gorge country with dark clustered pines in the drainage seams. Up ahead on the top acreage were flat meadows packed with gnarled salt-air brush. It was good grouse cover in the fall. I drove and thought about the grouse and the cold air turning to iron in my chest.

"Right about the time the picnic flies start walking on water," Hawley said. "The salmon have to wait off the sandbar until the river shoots a hole, first rain."

"Picnic flies. I call them sweat-biters."

"That's because you work outdoors, Doyle."

"Tell me something I don't know."

"Stop the truck. See down there?" He pointed below the highway.

"It's just pasture."

"Yeah, it's hard to see. Twenty years ago there were railroad boxcars in that field. When the sun hits just right you can see the impressions."

I drove again, steered around a cutback that brought the mill into view. It was lunch hour for the regular crew, they were down on their tailgates. And the laid-offs, the guys looking to patch into a shift, stood in groups at the edge of the yard. I thought how owing a buddy is one thing, but a buddy out of work, that's heaping shit on manure.

"After I got kicked out of the Coast Guard I lived a year in one of those boxcars," Hawley said.

"Hippie camp?"

"Boy, the full range of strange. Women ran it. The men had to keep to the boxcars until the women summoned us up to the main house, one at a time."

"Sounds all right."

"They'd make a man do a bunch of work around the place and then sit him down in a wooden chair and shave his beard, send him back."

"But it fell apart."

"Kids from San Francisco hitched north, couldn't figure out why the guy in a ball cap and shitkickers was yelling at them, cut your hair and get a job. Talk about free love, more times than not, ends up a bunch of rednecks playing stinky-finger behind the barn. No offense."

I hit the brakes for a flatbed parked crosswise on the narrow road. "Read the map," I said.

"Tanner Cr. Br."

A man in a purple jacket got out of the flatbed, adjusting his belt. He didn't much look in our direction. His jacket was a high school letter jacket, felted wool with leather sleeves short in the arms. It said CHAVEZ on the back, but the man was white. He stopped on Hawley's side, keeping back in the shade edge of the creek cut.

"What's doing?" Chavez said.

I told him how I planned to summer the sheep on the top acreage to the BLM line.

"Make another plan," he said. He reached into his jacket as if to tuck his shirt. "Plenty of other places to run your sheep."

"It's good country," Hawley said.

Chavez acted like he didn't hear. He looked over his shoulder where the ballast bit the hill. "Not this year," he said. "This year it ain't so good. Might wanna turn around and forget it."

Sun lit up the dash and windshield. I had to squint to see Chavez in the shade.

"Turnaround's up past the bridge," Hawley said and tapped the quadrangle.

"My first job out of Quentin had me sorting bolts in a warehouse near Sacramento," Chavez said. "In there with a guy named Skaggs. Skaggs and me agreed on one thing: when a bolt hits a scale pan it makes a particular sound. A truck transmission dropped into Reverse."

I pushed the clutch and worked the gearshift.

"There it is," said Chavez. He tossed some bills on the dash. "I know our livelihood sort of rubs up against yours."

I woke in my jeans in the middle of the night from a dream of the Pit River Revival, where I watched a girl in a two-piece ride the rope swing, the dingy knot squeezed into her crotch fold. The oaks bleeding sap, a thin golden rain spangling in the sun. The first time he said it: "Don't get

what's in your head confused with good sense."

The bonfire burned to brands, the generator gave out, Dave Hawley shook me. "Come get your friend," he said. "The golden boy. He's finished throwing up."

Bill Scobie lay naked on the gunnysacks of wool. He was painted gold head to toe, including his pump handle withered in the cold. "They wanted to see the great seal," Hawley said. "I had a gallon of gold left over. They found it." We lifted Bill into his own truck, and I slid behind the wheel, lit the bankment highway. Even in the dark, I knew the barracks, the tent camps, the briny backwater waited out there beyond the cones of light.

Marlene came out of the house, and I cranked the radio to wake Bill.

"More high-end torque means more towing capacity," Marlene said, sounding just like the radio. "That's what I need—what we all need—more towing capacity. More capacity in general."

"I'll walk back," I said. "What's it, a couple miles?"

I watched them move behind the Visquine. Bill tried to stand, and sat down again in the kitchen chair. Marlene began, with a basin and cloth, to scrub away the paint, while Bill talked—no doubt about what he'd seen in the barn. Hawley's version: the goddess of wisdom driving her spear into the grizzly bear, the ships in the harbor turned oil platforms, the gold miner clipping buds of marijuana. "Fuck the commission. I'll be chain-sawing Chiefs for the tourist trap in Myers Flat, either way."

I woke again in the watery light. The old goose-down cover slid halfway off the steel-spring cot. Fog pushed through the porch screen's salt-crusted weft. Clung silver beads, got that way with my breathing, and each one held the yard, the fence line, the highway. Years ago: "That's right, son. A hundred different worlds, and you live in one of them—or do you?"

Steph was in the kitchen frying eggs. I watched her through the quarreled back door. She stood in her robe on the linoleum, her hip cocked the way some women stand to hold a baby. She had the oven cracked to stave chill. I thought, go in there, man—eat those eggs with ketchup and bread, make her fry two more. Instead, I beat it off the porch and cranked the hose valve, worked the water through my straggle to my scalp, the cold binding in my shoulders. I cupped handfuls under my arms and drank straight from the bit.

The fog blew in off the beach, crusting up on the hill fringe, like it does before a squall. I walked up to the barn and stood in the man-door. Dave Hawley lowered himself to a knee-squat and took up a fist of spoil—wood chips and shavings. "Never liked to work in relief," he said. He stayed in the barn while a crew of men rolled the seal out of the double doors, leaned it upright on the forks of a log truck, and winched it down with canvas straps.

"Mamma put the cornstarch in this one," the trucker said. He flashed his high beams into the pasture, where the grass snapped and heaved in gusts of wind. Hawley shook my hand and climbed into the cab.

"I want to see the look on the governor's face," he said.

I went over the crank job one more time, checking the winch buckles and chocks. I thumbed the driver in the side-view, and he chuffed the flap-stack, graveled down the road, and left me alone with the storm coming in dark over the marsh and the salt grass dunes. I watched the truck clover onto 101, exhaust plumes drafting down off the stack, blooming red in the brake lights. The great seal of the state of California turned in the fog, showing its face, a giant wooden coin. Call it in the air. Tails.

THE MAN WHO MARRIED A TREE

by TONY D'SOUZA

I.

THE TOWNSMEN

Once there was this man, came one day to our town. Drank in the bar evenings, kept to himself. He had India ink tattoos of tigers on his forearms. Some people guessed he'd been a sailor, seen the tragedies that ocean-faring men do, that's why he didn't talk. Got drunk one night finally, passed out with his boots on in the scrap of wood by the river next to the bridge where the trains run over it. Right there in the middle of things where everyone could see. Maybe it was a cry for help, who knows? The sheriff put him in the tank the night and he mumbled about those tigers, and bad weather. Didn't go into the bar again after that. Must have sobered him up, settled his spirit here.

Ours is a good town. Trains come through a few times a day, hauling coal north and lumber south. They stop our pickups at the crossing and we contemplate the garish, foreign graffiti painted by angrier people than we are on the cars as they rumble by. Up on the mountain is a tower, but cellular phones don't work down here. What's being said by all those invisible voices bouncing around in the sky? Tourists stop in for goods and

gas, talking about this and that from the city, telling us how beautiful our home place is, then they go on. Our young people move on, too. We remain, our stories with us.

But that man who came, he built a quiet place for himself down past the south end; built the cottage by hand, sent some business the hardware store's way awhile, then that was it; he lived out by the trees. Trees everywhere about that place; he spent his time among them. Grew corn and vegetables; he fished and hunted. Got to know those trees real well. Then he married one.

None of us went to the wedding; no one was invited. But it's said he wore a sharp military uniform of some foreign design, brown, with a saber at his side and a few polished medals on his breast. He wasn't young anymore, though his beard had dark streaks of life in it, and the tree wasn't either, though she was lovely. Her limbs were long and lithe, black spiders spun gossamer webs about her crown for a veil. Now and again someone would catch a glimpse of her standing by herself back by their bend of the creek, her pinnacle bent like thinking, her leaves hanging over the water like long straight hair and her man not around. It was the water and the stones and her solitude that did it, but she stood there like a Japanese poem. Didn't know how to feel just then: those who saw her spoke of embarrassment, of feeling like they'd stumbled upon a beautiful woman taking a quiet bath. She was a tree that made you consider other trees, the trees that cover the mountains around here in their green and silent multitudes. Trees, trees everywhere. A wide and unknown world of trees bearing down on you when you paused to think.

Even so, when the wedding was first getting rumored, some of the womenfolk got their feathers up. They complained about it at the Elks, at the Eagles. They said, 'Now every Tom, Dick, and Harry is going to think he can up and run off with a tree.' We just shrugged our shoulders and looked at one another over our beers. Even if in our hearts of hearts we wanted to, who's to say there was a tree out there for us? For a while after that, you'd hear about this fella or that going off for a long walk in the woods, about how his wife or girlfriend had marched out there to haul him back in. But as far as actually marrying a tree? Time went by and no one else ever did.

Maybe we should have, though no one ever says it. Maybe that would have shaken up the tired order around here.

II.

THE POSTMAN

After that queer character who married a goddanged tree got old as folk and died, his sister breezed into town, stayed awhile in that heap of a cottage he'd tossed up. What was his disorder anyway? A lost zip, if you ask me. But she was a savvy, skinny number from the city, pretty sorta around the eyes, you could tell right away she'd seen her share: she smoked. She sat mornings in the rocking chair on the porch and rocked and smoked and looked out at the trees where they stood just beyond his garden. Never once was so much as a circular for that place, but I went by anyway when she came to town. I wore long pants those hot days, so she wouldn't see my chicken legs and count me out right away. I've been around long enough to know you never can tell what might arrive with the mail.

Three days running I went up to the gate, said as polite as can be, 'Howdy-do, miss,' then rummaged through my sack as though I might actually have something for that pathetic address. What a joke! But I've fooled enough lonely housewives in my day not to try. Then I'd shake my head at her and say, 'Seems like sorry again, dear. Got nothing for you today. Go figure. Get twenty in a day and then nothing for a month.' On the fourth day, she puffed a long plume of smoke out my way as I came up the walk, and before I could say word one, she said, 'Ask your question, postman, and let's be done with it.'

Well now. Well just you a minute now. But I'm too quick not to make the best of anything. I hung my old wrists on the pickets of that fence like it was any old day or place and it was time to talk. I looked out the corner of my eye at some dandelions for courtesy, and then I said, 'Since you put it that way. There's been rumors running around for a long while, rumors about your brother. It's said he was married here, but you never did see any wife puttering about the place.'

'Oh he was married all right. Happily goddamned married. He married a tree. Didn't ask any of us neither. Just went off and did it. A common trash lot birch.'

I leaned in then, said like whispering, 'Seems like I'd heard that, yep. A birch. The white kind. But since you brought it up, I'll say it doesn't sound exactly trash lot to me. Understand me now, the water's clean back there, comes from the Soda spring. City folks same as you come up every now and again with bottles, take our water back with them. It's a pride for folk around here.'

'Common here, common there, I've always said. A birch. Why not a maple or an oak? Why not something to make people proud? That was the problem with Henry. Always did do his own thing.'

'You mean to say it didn't surprise you people?'

'Surprise? Henry? Henry never had eyes for anything but trees. You take a bar full of leggy blondes and a tree walks in, and the next thing you know, there would be Henry, buying her a drink, asking all sorts of questions and embarrassing himself. He got tangled up with a knotty old buckthorn when we were kids. Mother had to clip him out of her brambles, and then she beat him. Threatened to chop that tree right down. But Henry got down on his knees and hugged the skinny trunk and said, 'Mama, don't you chop this sweet buckberry down because she's the only thing I ever loved.' He wasn't even but eleven, twelve. We knew before then. When he was little, before he could talk, he'd stand out in the yard with his arms up and his eyes closed, stock still for hours, acting like a full-grown sycamore, like he'd been charged with holding up the sky. I bet that's when that old buckthorn got her eye on him. Ruined him. Ruined him she did. What can you expect from an exotic? She so old and twisted, him like a shoot. It made us all sick.'

She swung her eyes on me, let out a slow cloud of smoke the way old Chinese ladies used to do in pictures. She said, 'Postman? Do you really want to know the truth? I'll tell you. I loved an elm. Loved him my whole life. He grew in the parkway beyond our sidewalk, and I spent hours peeking at him from my bedroom window. Loved him more and more with every beat of my heart. How strong he used to be, so serene and bold! But I never worked up the courage to tell him. I used to be shy. And I was scared. What if he didn't love me as much as I loved him? All that longing, all those years! The Dutch disease got him. They sawed him down, chipped him to dust. Wrecked my life. Wrecked it as thoroughly as anything.'

Well then. Felt like someone'd slapped me. She looked at those trees, and I did, too. They stood at the edge of the yard like watching, like they'd been listening to what we'd said, like they'd been thinking about who we were as people. Gave me the creeps. Made me want to get out of there and never go back. I tipped my cap to her and hurried down the way. Didn't look back either. Made me think a second; made me think about all that paper folded in all those letters.

III.

THE HARDWARE STORE OWNER

Didn't want nails, that one. Don't know if that's good or bad. Joined everything. That's finer work than using nails. So that's good. But money spent on nails would have been appreciated around here, so that's bad. Who in the world is supposed to know? But he knew his tools and what he wanted to do. Bought his chisels and mortar and lumber and glass and that was it, nothing spendy.

Thing is, lots of fellas don't like to talk, not wanting to talk can't tell you everything there is to know about 'em. Why one guy came in here for years buying shovels. Every couple of months he'd come in, pick out a shovel, pay for it, go. Just like that. Never so much as hello. The next thing you know he's got Fish and Game out there putting up 'Wetland' signs. Built an eleven-acre marsh out there. Dug it himself. By hand. A couple guys went out and saw it. Said the whole place was nuts with buffleheads and mergansers.

Them tigers, too. The pictures guys put on their arms only say so much. Seen stranger tattoos than them tigers. Saw one guy with a tattoo of a flying pig. His old lady only'd let him wear shoes in the house when pigs could fly, on account of her carpet. He got old, and winter got to his ankles, and that was that.

In the end, we did sell that fella some nails. At least to his sister. She paid his expenses and they needed a bunch to tack the lid on the pine box they put him in. Know a lot of people around here, but didn't know him. Would have liked to, if he'd of had the mind for it. Would have passed the time.

IV.

THE SHERIFF

I may have been the only one around these parts ever did shake his hand. Was in the morning, wasn't it? Yes, when I locked him up that night for a 647-F, Public Intoxication. Sleeping in the wood by the creek. I knew he was there that whole time. Fine by me. Then some old lady or other phoned in, woke me from a nod. Don't mind nodding now and again since I lost my Mary. 'Sheriff! Sheriff!' she whispered. 'There's a drunk man making mischief by the creek. That old sailor. Let 'em run loose at night, sheriff, a lady's liable to have all sorts of sorrows come calling. Why, what if he gets up and starts over here on those big, thick legs of his? What could happen then? Him so brawny and all, and me just like a baby bird? I'll tell you. He could kick down my door like sticks. He could throw me on my bed like a rag doll and force himself on me. Could you imagine it? Me all alone for the taking and him so strong? He could do just whatever he pleased with that big hulk of a body of his. Been watching him from my window for over an hour. He's a bad one, a bad one sure. Better do something quick before he gets on over here and takes advantage.'

What can you do when the whole town signs your paycheck? I took up a pair of cuffs, my gun, the keys, the whole rigamarole. When I got down there, he was snoring like a baby with the low branches of those trees hanging down on him strange-like, like a blanket, like the trees had wanted to keep him warm. 'Hey now, bud,' I said to him and nudged his elbow with the toe of my boot, 'can't sleep here, fella. Got a nice bed for you though if you come along.' Took a while, but I roused him. Mumbled about the weather at first like an old drunk lost soul. They fall off the train. It's like one single man, over and over and over again. Something fundamentally wrong with the world when it breeds all these lost dudes. But he was polite enough when his eyes got to blinking. Got to his feet as best he could, wasn't ashamed to use my shoulder for a steady. Saw my badge, things came clear. Said to me, 'Sorry, officer.'

'It's sheriff. And there ain't no sorry in this world.'

'I know it,' he said back to me, 'but I'll say it anyway.'

Then he moved his feet as nicely as a kitten. Big fella, too, so I was glad for it. A clean one, clean hands, he smelled of the woods and pines. Didn't have any reason to put the bracelets on him.

Folk keep their eye on the new one in town. They could have said a word to him now and again on the street, in the hardware store, but you know folk. They call it 'leaving a man to his business.' For a while, they liked to talk about him in conversation, wondering who he was, his tattoos, his last night in the bar. Folk is always the same. Natural curiosity. Nothing much else to occupy them around here, liable even to craft a story or two; they'd do it to anybody. He built a reasonable place down past the south end, gave it a gabled roof, put in windows just as smart as a glazier. I swung by now and again to see that he complied with our ordinances. He did. I'd wave to him if he was around. That was it. Never had a problem with him again. Wish the whole valley could be like that. His passing touched me, I'll own to it. Always hate to see a good man go, makes you count your own time, even if you're ready.

I remember that morning, the morning I let him out. Sitting on the bed and waiting for me, his big hands in his lap just like his mama taught him. I gave him his pebbles back, the pine needles he'd had in his pockets. Then we shook hands. Felt the power in him, felt it right down through my bones. A strong man, and not just of the body. He could have made a fine man around these parts if he'd wanted. They say he married, so I reckon he did.

V.

THE SPINSTER

No justice in this world, if you ask me. None. Nose to the grindstone since the day I was born. Nobody walked the line like me. Nary so much as a peep. Spend the whole of this life minding my own and walking the line and waiting for my ship to come in and then you hear about someone running off and marrying a tree. How's a body supposed to react to all that?

Why my younger sister Becky, you should have seen. Had everything, she did. Drinking and cussing all those years away in the city. Liked lights, being under them, guess she thought she was something of a movie star the way she sought them out. And then she came back worn and spent if you ask me, lines all in her face, not like mine from patient age, the worn-out kind that come on a person all at once, make you look like a dried-up apple forgotten in the yard. She smelled funny, too. But Papa acted like it was the day she was born. Then that train supervisor who hopped off here a while, he dallied with me, I'll tell you. All Aggie this, Aggie that. Those were days, all right. Felt like I'd eaten bugs, the way my stomach fluttered when he'd come up in the evening in his overalls, whistling like it was going to rain gold. I even thought it might, too. 'Gimme a kiss, Aggie. One sweet little peck.' Dang near wrung me out with that. Next thing you know Becky shows up working her citified ways on him and he couldn't see me any longer the way you can't ever really look at coal. Just like that. Then he popped out with this tin ring like he'd found a quarter and put it in a gumball machine, and Papa was wont to kill a calf and Mama sewed Becky a trousseau on the bias. Moved back to the city, those two did. Had seven kids. Their faces were always dirty, even in photographs. I bet they let them eat molasses.

When the man with the tigers came, I'd see him walking up to the bar from my window. Walked right by here every night: a clock on two legs. I'd watch him go by and then I'd sit down to my programs. I'd knit a bit and watch my shows, and then it would be time to see him go by again on his way home, to see if he was really as regular as he was making out. And for a while, he was. 'A drinker, Aggie,' my quilting ladies warned. I blushed and said, 'Bet I could fix him.' Even waved to him once. Just lifted up my hand on some crazy urge and waved it at him. He didn't even nod his head.

The next thing you know he's stumbling around in the bracken like any of them zombies fall off the train. So he wasn't what I'd made him out to be after all. Can't a man even acknowledge a lady when she condescends to lift her hand at him? Maybe he couldn't see me with the light out and me behind the curtain and all, but then again, shouldn't he of just felt it? Shouldn't he have simply known?

All these people in the world wanting a little something for themselves: he goes off and marries a tree. Could she cook? Could she clean? These are the questions I'd like answered. Against the way of things, if you ask me. The world so big and lonesome, and he marries a tree. Why that's a rejection of the way life is, a basic desire to not participate. What's next? People marrying rocks? Mud? Did she ever knit him a pair of tartan socks? That's what I'd like to know.

A good man, that's what they're saying now that it's too late to say anything else. Simple enough for people to temper their judgments when a man's just passed on. But ask them when nobody's looking, ask them what they really think. A good man? Just go and ask anyone normal.

VI.

THE FOREST SERVICE SURVEYOR

Had to go out there, tagging trees. Had a hammer, nails, my uniform on, my badge. Had a plate. Number 5393. Just doing my job, surveying, been doing it for years. Sure, they'll use my work to make maps that they'll sell to the timber industry, but a man has to feed his family, put his kids through school, help his kids feed their kids and put them through school, and so on and so on. No way around that. That's the way the world works. Still, working around trees all the time just seems to change your perception. Can't think of anything nicer than a tree.

Anyway, while I was back there looking at his tree, the man came charging out from nowhere. I knew him even if he didn't know me. Everybody knew him. That's what happens when you marry a tree. He says to me, 'Can I help you, mister?' those tigers flexing on his arms like stretching, like waking up. I say, 'I got to put this plate on this tree. Marking boundaries, you know.' He gives me a good, hard, long look. He says, 'Do what you've got to do. But understand something. That's my wife.' We just looked at each other a while. Two months before my stinking retirement and I had to deal with that. What was I going to do? Have two old guys like us splashing around in the creek and fistfighting over a tree? I walked down and nailed that plate to an old cherry. Who cares, right? The line's still straight, more or less. Maybe they'll even leave that hollow alone for a while. But what I want to know is, what gave that one single guy the right to go and mess with the rules? We all love trees, don't we? Why couldn't he have married some tree on his own damned property?

VII.
THE SODA CREEK

He was a good man, he left the fish alone. That is to say, he took one once in a while, without game or folly, the way bears do, ospreys. I liked running through the hair of his legs, his toes, he was clean even when he came to me to be cleaned. It's about the spirit of a man, cleanliness. I praise it in men as much as they praise it in me.

That first year, he took stones from my bed to build the foundation of his house. The deep spaces he left in me I filled, and the fish came to nest in those spaces in turn. He would come to me in the evening and smoke a cigarette and listen to me and mull over the things men like him have to. All he seemed to do at that time was think. Think and smoke and listen to me as he looked at the evening. What advice did I give him that I don't give to any man? Once in a while he would bury his feet in the dirt on the bank and close his eyes as though to grow, to become a tree himself, and I would eddy up and rinse the dirt away. If he had been a child, I would have had a heart for that. But he was old enough to understand well that it was his sentence to be a man. What would it be after all if the squirrels began leaping out of the tall pines as though they were jays, if the jays used their wings to climb?

And her? I knew her from a seed. Knew her whole stand, generations of them. Sturdy trees; they held and died and made that bank. A fire came through one dry year and we all had to learn that even when life has seemed to stop, it will start again. What a fine young tree she had been, standing in a riotous clump with her brothers and sisters, taut in the wind, graceful as a wand. After the fire, she was the only one who came back, hardened.

He'd seen some things. She had seen plenty, too. It happened slowly, befitting their natures. This pleased me because what do I have but time? Though those first years he would not admit to himself his love for the tree, he came to sit at me where he could see her out of the corner of his eye. It was as though he wished at all times to know how she fared, without admitting to himself that he needed to know. He'd scratch his arm and look at me, as though she was just another stick to him. For her part, what was the man to her? What was anything? She had lost much: her kin before the fire, the landscape that had held her before the loggings. She had survived to see the mountains dressed again in sturdy trees she'd watched sprout. The man sat and smoked on the bank until he knew my lie, every stone that riffled my run, the new currents I'd form when I'd grow restless and shift. All the time he was looking at her without turning his eyes. He was wondering, I imagine, if he had the strength to approach her, to be turned away by her, too.

Who determines these things? Winters came and went. The turtles burrowed beneath my knowing to dream their unknown winter dreams, emerging again after the ice had dripped from the tree branches and every part of me awoke. She was in full bud, glorious; of course he had seen it before. But perhaps he'd had a whisper of death that long winter, certainly he had streaks of winter in his beard. He approached the tree, finally, an evening when I was full of nymphs hatching into yellow clouds of newly winged damsels and causing the trout to leap from me as if for joy, and crossed that short expanse of stone and shade and soil that had separated them. He did not move on my bank in the stumbling, heedless stride of a buck, but in the measured pace of one with the age to know he cannot afford to fall again. With life awakening all about them in the world, he lay down at her roots and rested his head gently against her base. As simple as that. What a moment that was! I would have stopped myself in my eternal trickle if only to let them know how tense I was, how much I needed, then, to know. All the woods fell silent for everything in them, too, had all been waiting for this moment. It seemed, suddenly, that so much depended on

this when we all knew that nothing depended on it at all: bird and otter and rock and moss. And as we held ourselves to see what she would do, even the wind paused her coursings. What did that tree do? What did that fine tree who had no need of anything from a man to prove the success of her stubborn existence do? She rustled her branches to cast her soft bud casings on him like down.

VIII.

THE SOIL

Mountains fear me, rocks. The stones in the rivers that traverse me fear me. Plants fear me, trees. Men fear me. I am everything's afterlife.

I would like to speak with my cousins. But mountains separate us, deserts. All will crumble and fall. Time belongs to me. Everything becomes me.

My voice is baritone. Only the mountains pay attention to what I say. I have been brutalized by man for twelve thousand years and still I remain. Divided, transplanted, shoveled, sold, and, finally, salted, I can only laugh, in my undulations. Even sidewalks will return to me, once the current tumult has subsided.

My reaches have seen much, have seen at the north of my body a man who loved a tree. What is there to say but this: he warmed me with his body, the length of him upon me, lying at her roots. I knew what was happening and I did not care. Why should I? His body would return to me, and so would his tree.

But he walked upon me in his bare feet. And he lay upon me at her roots. Her roots were strong, like a web that wound through me, her smallest tendrils searching and holding onto her life. But after they had married, the man would come and lay his short expanse upon me, and I would warm, what choice or care did I have? And the warmth of him would warm and open her roots, and then she would take the minerals suspended in me. For twelve thousand years, man has worried about my development. But the man who loved the tree let his warmth seep through me. This opened her roots and insisted upon her growth. These vibrations between them I hadn't otherwise known. I haven't needed to; I am a being that eats everything. This between the man and the tree was a new thing to me: tender in its quietness; I will admit their love.

IX.
THE RED-TAILED HAWK

Marriage? No. But net me, feed me, love me for a time, and I will feed us both. Let me go. My love is for myself. Things revolve, as I see them. I don't condemn them, don't care to understand them. Wind in my feathers as I surveyed them from my perch; all of creation has its particular way.

X.
THE RACCOON, THE POSSUM, THE PIGEON, THE SKUNK

We love men, could love the man who'd feed us.

XI.
THE TROUT

Grub, grub.

XII.
THE MOUNTAIN

I've seen stranger.

XIII.
THE FORESTS

We've seen worse.

XIV.
TELEPHONE POLES

If only. If only.

XV.
DEATH

I wait. I win.

XVI.
THE CORONER

The Hutchinson girl found him. Having trouble with that girl, her folks were, trouble keeping her out of the woods. Those woods seem to pull her in like a magnet. They made her lead me to where the body was at the tree's roots. The tree had shaken her leaves down to cover him and he seemed no worse for the wear. I had half a notion to let him lie right there. But the news had already gotten out and things aren't done that way around here. It took a handful of strong backs to lift him out. On the table I opened him up and found what I'd guessed: thrombosis.

I wear the mortician's hat in this little town; I'm also the undertaker. I put on my black coat and went to his cottage to have a look and see if I couldn't find a way to contact any kin. It was a windy evening, and there were leaves blowing all around the place. The door didn't even have a lock on it, and inside, there were hand-painted pictures of all the birds of this region, and an easel, and quite a number of well-thumbed books, in stacks. Just any sort of book you could imagine reading. How had he got them there? Where had he come from anyway? There was a letter stuck in one of them, old and yellowed, a handwritten thing wishing him well in the Middle East, signed, 'Your loving sister.' That's how we found her. A pleasant lady, her brother's passing touched her the way it was supposed to.

'What would you like to do with the body?' I asked her an evening after some time had passed and she'd settled in. The priest and deacon had been nosing around, but she said he wouldn't have wanted any of that, he wouldn't have wanted anything. So we stood in that house surrounded by his simple things, not knowing what to do and looking at each other. It was one of those long moments when there's nothing you can do but look away at the wall and feel terrible for people you don't even know. Before I could ask the question again, there was a knock at the door. 'Oh,' she said, startled. 'Who could that be? Maybe that idiot postman?' She opened the door to reveal a solemn gathering of townsfolk, the men thumbing their hats in their hands, the women in coats for the cold. The sheriff was before them all and he cleared his throat, looked up at her from where he'd been looking down, and said, 'We know we've been lax about things, but we'd like to welcome you to our town, and offer our condolences.'

'Thank you,' she said simply, and I felt a welling up inside of me for the basic goodness of my own people. There were leaves falling on everyone's shoulders, and we all looked around and noticed it was autumn.

'We'd like to help you any way we can,' he told her, and she nodded her head at them. That was all, the saying of the things that are supposed to be said, the acknowledgment of them. The moment passed and they turned to leave. She looked at me a second urgently as though something large had crossed her mind and then she called to them. 'Wait! I don't have a place to

bury my brother. It doesn't seem right to take him away, and the ridiculous law says I can't bury him here.'

They came back in their dark coats, murmuring to one another, a crowd of people, people with their hearts turned in kindness. The sheriff cleared his throat again, said, 'We'll take him. We didn't much know him, but then again, maybe we did. He lived here a long time. We'll put him in our cemetery as one of our own.'

The service was simple, a few words from the sheriff, then she read a poem about a tree losing its leaves. Instead of a marker, they planted a sapling, a willow. The sister went back to wherever she came from with his effects, and spiders got comfortable in his house.

One day, before the snows came, a feeling came over me, and I drove out to his place. Things were changing there, the grass was tall between the dried cornstalks, leaves were everywhere in piles. The land was taking the house and garden back. There was a worn path leading back to the creek, and I followed it, followed it back until I found her, his birch, standing in her height by the edge of the water. I cannot explain what came over me. An old feeling that had been lost inside me long ago in the course of this profession, I felt it suddenly looking at her loneliness. I took off my glove, placed my hand on her bark, and told her as honestly as I could, 'I'm sorry.'

I know it didn't mean much. Sorrow, death. What are any of us in the face of it? I stood there with her until darkness fell all over the face of the land. It was the least I could do. It comforted me.

TERMINAL

by J. ERIN SWEENEY

SAY A RISING movie star visited a children's hospital and a little boy fell in love with her and decided that she was his destiny. Say the nature of his disease mattered. Say it also mattered that she had received no guarantees about the future of her professional success. Say the industry is fickle. Say bad things can happen to innocent people. Say good things, too. Say the story ends neither happily nor sadly because it is not always the privilege of stories to know when they are about to end, are ending, or have ended.

Say the movie star looks over a small sea of small faces and decides that, as there is a time for every purpose under heaven, it is now time for humility. The movie star is a sensitive person in many ways and this realization has the power to crush some of her composure. But not all of it, and she is in the act of curbing the humility in order to salvage the remaining composure as her eyes move to the boy. She places her long hand on his head. On the side of his head, rather, and the back of it. She is both caressing the boy—humility—and pushing him away in order to stabilize herself in a world of complex and unanswerable questions. Many of the questions are sad. The boy has no hair and his scalp is smooth and warm.

She is surprised at how alive it feels, in spite of everything.

* * *

Consider this: that every time a last thought is repeated, a story comes to an end. People need clarity, and that is what stories are for. Our own lives are complicated—nothing is ever resolved because nothing is ever over. But stories end, so they can be pure. The joy is pure and the suffering is pure and even the questions that can't be answered are precise and clear.

A lost dog has finally found his family, and they're shouting his name and they hold their arms out and he jumps into them...

It is the end of an argument, and they are more in love than ever...

The criminal has been caught at last, and punishment is waiting...

Here is the baby, born finally, healthy, and the mother is sweaty but she's okay too...

These are ends, but they are also beginnings, and in life they will end and begin again and again. Every time something happens a world of possible action opens up, and possible meanings. But in fiction every story is an end, because we are only reading the end. Its last notes are sonorous and beautiful and final. They are beautiful. They are final.

Say a marriage is tragic. Say that the people close to the couple can find no words for the things they have done. Say at every point where the body of the world touches their bodies, people have bad dreams and lose their faith and turn their eyes away from things they once trusted. Even if this is true, it doesn't matter: it isn't the end.

There is a journalist standing behind the movie star. The journalist watches the movie star touch the boy's head and recognizes this gesture for exactly what it is: a lucky person surrounded by the unlucky and in the midst of a vanishing revelation. The journalist knows better than to try to articulate this in a one-paragraph piece for a glamour magazine so shallow that its appeal is limited even among its target audience of middle-class preteens. So he will keep his thoughts to himself. He will use the paragraph simply to praise her humanity.

The journalist speaks later to a little girl, one who had been standing beside the caressed boy with the naked scalp.

"Would you say," prompts the journalist, "that she is as kind as she is beautiful?"

"Yes," says the little girl.

The journalist waits. He touches his notepad with the tip of his pen.

"She is as kind as she is beautiful," says the little girl.

The journalist smiles. So does the girl.

They are satisfied with their work and with each other. Both of them have the same thought: it has been a good day.

Meanwhile, the little boy makes a decision. He will marry her.

Every part of the little boy, and every part of the rest of the world that touches a part of him, has aligned behind a single purpose. His decision is as true as any he has ever made. He will marry her. He will marry her. He will marry her.

GOD AND THE COCONUTS

by SARAH RAYMONT

WHEN GOD GAVE me my own island, He said, take this island and make it yours. Do whatever you want, He said. Invite anyone and drink all the booze there is. But there's one caveat, you must never take the coconuts from the tree with the purple trunk. I asked him why, but He had already vanished into a plume of smoke.

So the weekend came around and I invited all my friends. I told them to invite all their friends, so I'd say there was a fair amount of people looking to have their fun on my island. Before I started passing around the liquor and fish that I'd spent all day catching, citrus-marinating in the sun, and grilling, I clapped my hands together and called everyone "gang." "Hey gang," I said, and told them to run wild in the place, to get freaky with each other but stay away from the coconuts from the tree with the purple trunk. I said it twice and then I made them repeat it back to me. We turned it into a song and some music executive in the crowd suggested we record it. He said, let me just pull out my DAT recorder here and rig up the satellite phone so I can send it back to the studio. This got everyone very excited and the booze started going around. The chorus was a rousing one and the lyrics were jubilance mixed with profundity. People brought

their own experiences to the song but we made our own sound. We worked very hard. The younger people gathered sticks and beat them together. The older people clapped their hands, smiling meaningfully out of their mouths and eyes in that way that only old people can. Everyone was sweating.

By the time the fish was eaten, the sky was dark, and we lit the sticks on fire. This left us without percussion, so I designated myself to round up more sticks. I left the group and trudged alone through sand, leaving the happy fireplace smoldering behind me. The waves yelled secrets into shore and the stars batted their eyes my way. I hummed a tune reminiscent of the song I imagined they were still singing back at the fire. I was pretty keen on getting back because new lines were hitting me with every step. So when I reached up and grabbed the first dark shape I could knock on, I had no idea what it was attached to. It was night after all. God didn't illuminate the trees on the island for me. And purple is only a few shades away from black. But the minute I pulled the coconut off there was the most enormous crack of lightning I have ever seen or heard. It was so loud and bright that they all must have heard it, and were wondering, what the hell? I wanted to run back and soothe them, tell them I was okay, but I was pretty alarmed, not to mention disappointed in myself because I knew I'd let them all down. But I knew that I wouldn't be seeing that gang of music makers again. And in that minute, I was struck with the greatest lyrics of all time.

God was pretty ticked off that I did exactly what He said not to do. I knew He was going to go into the whole Adam and Eve bit and so straight off I told Him to spare me. I told Him, cut to the chase God, and let's make this as painless as possible. I said either send me back to the party so I can drop my rhyme, or get it over with and knock me off. God seemed a little taken aback by my forwardness (as was I), but I explained to Him that when good words come to you, you just want to get someplace where you can get them down. It isn't often that large groups of people get together and then produce sound so true, sound so raw, that it actually means something. I tried to calm down so that I'd appear reasonable. I said, God, if You kill me, at least let me write down my lines so You can take them back to the party, or send a seabird or something if You feel You can't show Your face. Not only did I set the parameters for my punishment but I accepted them wholeheartedly.

I could tell that I won: God was flummoxed. As kindly as I could, I told Him that people aren't as dumb as He thinks. I told Him that maybe He should have more faith in us and yes, it was pretty dumb of me to go right to the one thing He told me to steer clear of. But God, I said, a purple tree? A snake? I said I'd help him come up with something else, something synthetic perhaps. I told Him that as men are drawn to nature, that He made us together, perhaps if He wants to keep something for Himself (and what God wanted those coconuts for I have no idea, but I'll let Him have a modicum of privacy), I suggested a nuclear reactor. I said, I for one wouldn't want to go in one of those in search of percussion. I suggested He get off the whole temptation thing anyway, that it's a real waste of time, and why not try songwriting for a creative outlet. I think He was pretty inspired, because He let me go, just like that. He walked down the beach the other way, without any speed to His steps. Perhaps He wanted me to see Him thinking, otherwise He'd have left in the smoke that He arrived in.

By the time I reached the roaring party and all the guests, I had already planned what I would say when I snuck up on them. And by the time I tipped my toes through the sand and roared, just as planned, "have no fear, gang: I am here!" the damnedest thing happened. I forgot my lines. But the gang was so happy to see those beat makers in my arms that it was only I who suffered the loss.

THE BIG DUD

by JACK PENDARVIS

DUDLEY DURDEN, 50, WAS the only reporter for the Lumber Land *Monitor* in Lumber Land, Alabama, a pine mill town owned historically by the Cuff family. His boss was 22, a concubine named Farrah with blond dreadlocks and a Chinese tattoo, property of the last remaining Cuff, bought and paid for with baubles and such. The newspaper office, located in a detached, early-twentieth-century private railroad car, sat like a gazebo on the Cuff family homestead.

Dud checked in with Farrah every Monday morning.

"Any assignments this week?"

"Nope."

"Can I pick up my paycheck?"

"It's right there in front of you."

"Turns out the eczema's spread to my eyeballs," said Dud.

"Mm," said Farrah.

"Well, not my eyeballs, don't panic. My eyelids. Can you see it?"

"Nope."

"I've got a cream for it. Store-bought."

"I'm doing something important," said Farrah. Dud looked. She was

tracing her hand with magic marker on a piece of yellow construction paper.

"I think the cream's helping," said Dud. "Sure you can't see it?"

The pink tip of Farrah's tongue was showing as she concentrated on finishing the outline.

"You know what I thought?" said Dud. "I thought I was scratching my jock itch and then accidentally touching my eyes. I thought I had jock eye. I really shouldn't complain. I don't even know if it's eczema. I diagnosed myself. Anyway, compared to my poor wife's skin, the skin she had when she was alive, I've got it easy. Only I don't have it easy. I keep hanging up the phone with my cheek."

Farrah held up her construction paper and squinted at it. Dud could see that the magic marker had gone through and ruined the desk, but Farrah didn't seem to notice or care. "Did you know you can make a Thanksgiving turkey using this method?" she said. "If it was Thanksgiving I'd show you how. See, that's what we would call an *interesting topic*."

Dud laughed politely. "Anyhoo, as I was saying, there's an off button right there on the receiver and my cheek keeps pushing on it when I talk. My cheek hangs up on people, isn't that funny? Last night I was eating potato chips and one of them was really hard and I thought, what if one of my teeth fell out? You know, broke off. I imagine it would look kind of like the inside of a peanut M&M with the peanut missing."

The phone buzzed, the intercom from the Big House.

"Thank God," said Farrah.

She said Three needed to see him.

Three was his private-eye name. His real name was Lombard Cuff III. He and Farrah lived in a fantasy world as far as Dud was concerned, where Three was a tough guy ferreting out big cases and his best gal Farrah was a champion of freedom of the press.

Dud pocketed his paycheck and headed across the big, dewy lawn to the mansion.

Three met him in the back doorway, wearing some kind of yellow suit that rich people wore. It looked so fruity and cheap that you'd have to be rich to wear it, in Dud's humble opinion.

"There he is!"

Three led Dud to the library, where the wisdom of ages stood floor-to-ceiling and a sideboard glittered with bottles. Three went over to pour drinks.

"Grab yourself one of those monster leather chairs the color of boeuf à la fucking bourguignon. You won't fucking believe it. They're so fucking soft you could cut them with a spoon. Damn, I must be hungry! You want some scotch?"

"Yes, please," said Dud.

"Neat?"

"If that's the way it's preferable. I wouldn't know."

"I could put a bow tie on it, is that neat enough? Hey, I thought I told you to sit."

Three had turned from the sideboard to catch Dud brooding along the endless spines.

"Oh, ha ha! That's great!" said Three. "I get it. You're looking for that thing you stapled together and gave me for Christmas. Sorry, this is where we keep the *real* books. No, I'm just fucking with you."

That *thing* was a reminiscence of my youth, thought Dud, full of rich details such as scuppernong arbors and dirt roads and the kindness of your forebears toward a young creative type with potential. And I had to go all the way to the archives in Mobile to get historical photos for Xeroxing.

But for Three it was just another occasion for hurtful comments that he probably imagined as wry.

Dud remembered being in the train car that day when Three kept holding up his hand to shush him because a commentator was talking about How Your Plants Seem to Die No Matter How Much You Water Them. Then Three explained to Dud and Farrah why the little verbal essay had been so fucking wry—he said "fucking wry" about two hundred times. After that he made them listen to a program where sarcastic men and women with soft voices tried to use various words in sentences. Three was extraordinarily drunk because earlier that day two of his bloodhounds had fallen out of an airplane and he was sad about it. He played along with the radio contestants, screaming every time he messed up, like it was the radio's fault. Then the nasal local announcer came on and said to stay tuned because he'd "be right Bach." Three was so thrilled by how "fucking clever" it was he tried to call and donate $10,000 in the name of his bloodhounds.

There was, Dud imagined, a multitude of coddled, civilized semi-drunks who found nothing more comforting than the weak puns and wretched insights of NPR.

Such was the intellect that had inherited this magnificent library.

"I guess you've read all these books," said Dud.

"Oh hell no. I just sit in here and drink and wait for a client to appear out of the fucking ether. Sometimes I'll pull out a fucking tome and take one look at the cover and put it right back. I get depressed."

"You should always judge a book by its cover," said Dud. What a comeback! It was way over Three's head.

"That's the spirit," said Three. He raised his glass. "Now come over here and let's drink to it."

Dud sat in the chair facing Three's and picked up his glass from the end table. The "scotch" made his eyes water with its terrible power and he couldn't even make the rim of the glass go all the way to his mouth from fear of gagging. So he mimicked taking a sip and put it back down.

Three moved his glass so he could get to the volume he had been using as a coaster. "Look. *How to Knit*. Isn't that fucking charming? Don't you think knitting would be a fucking great gimmick for a detective? I can just imagine myself working out the intricacies of a case in my mind, as the methodical clacking of my ivory needles lulls my faculties into a meditative fucking bliss. I've just about mastered the fucking chain stitch. Do you think it's gay?"

"Not in the sense you apparently mean. No, it's nice to have a hobby," said Dud.

"The thing is, I snagged a client somehow. Okay, she's a friend of the monsignor down in Bayou Cottard, you know, he was golfing buddies with the old man, and anyway... there's a thing I have to do, and Farrah doesn't want me going by myself—you know women."

"I was lucky enough to have a wife until she died."

"Right. Then you know what I'm talking about. What I'm putting on the table is, how would you like to earn the money I pay you for a change? You'd be like my goon."

"I've never envisioned myself as a goon, I'm sorry to say."

"Well, envision it, baby! It's not a term of fucking approbation. It's something detectives say. Like my right-hand man, that's all. Watching my back in case everything goes blooey. It's nothing strenuous. A stakeout. We probably won't even spot the guy."

"Well, in times of extreme quiet, such as I imagine a stakeout to be, there is a slight chance I could suffer from musical hallucinations. It's a

legitimate problem, documented in the *New Yorker* magazine if you don't believe me. I don't suffer from it chronically, to my knowledge, but there have been several times when I thought I might be on the verge. My ears have been clogged lately, and apparently the condition is exacerbated by the onset of deafness, from what I read in the *New Yorker* magazine."

Just as Dud expected, Three displayed no sense of recognition about the *New Yorker* magazine. His bourgeois mind was stuck somewhere at the National Public Radio level of discourse.

I bet I'm the only living being in Lumber Land that's even heard of the *New Yorker* magazine, Dud thought. But they don't want anything to do with you if you're not a so-called New Yorker.

There's this mime and this lady sitting in a fancy New York restaurant and they're holding hands across the table and the lady is saying to the mime, "We need to talk." Now that would make a damn fine cartoon. And nobody from the so-called *New Yorker* magazine even had the common courtesy to call me back. I'd like to see a better cartoon than that about a mime. Everybody hates mimes. I bet they laughed and laughed and then they said, Oh wait, this guy's from Alabama. No way we're cutting HIM a break. What does some JERK from ALABAMA know about MIMES? Only us sophisticated so-called New Yorkers are sophisticated enough to understand MIMES.

The scotch was tasting better now and though Three kept talking, Dud tuned him out in favor of more pleasant ruminations.

I bet I'm the only resident of Lumber Land, Alabama, who knows what a mime is, he thought.

You poor country hicks. It's a guy that doesn't talk.

Dud had another drink and contemplated some of his more promising ideas.

IDEA: Helicopter Island, the mysterious island that can only be reached by helicopter

IDEA: A serial killer who is brilliantly clever

IDEA: Winston Churchill

If a man is not liberal when he is young, etc. I believe Winston Churchill said that. If he is not a conservative when, etc. I believe I could be another Winston Churchill if I wasn't born in Alabama. Why the hell not? Nothing is impossible if you really try. Hold on to your dreams and they can come true. Miracles can happen in your daily life. All you have to do is look around. But whoever said that wasn't from Alabama.

Nobody thought much of Winston Churchill either, till he rose to a crisis. If I had a crisis I could rise to it. I can easily picture myself on a pile of rubble yelling, "I can hear you! And soon the terrorists will hear you!"

"So, are you with me?" said Three.

"As tempting as your offer is, I fear I may prove to be more of a liability than anything. Last night my right arm became completely numb for over twenty minutes. I don't want to speculate, but I can only assume it was some sort of reverse heart attack. Now, if you *really* think…"

"Look. Forget it," said Three. "I thought it would be cool."

2

Dud was sitting in his house, thinking about how embarrassing it would be to die there. He imagined some ambulance driver carefully picking his way through the squalor so as not to contract tetanus and saying something like, "Pee-yew! No wonder he died! What a dump!" and so on. Ambulance drivers and others acquainted with death on a daily basis were known to make just such sarcastic quips on supposedly solemn occasions.

The phone rang. Dud kicked around in the papers and junk on his floor, looking for it. Finally it stopped ringing.

About twenty minutes later, as darkness fell, Dud was still sitting there and a car pulled up outside. Dud's scalp vibrated. He puked up a little something but swallowed it down before it could get out of his mouth. Who was it? A maniac come to kill him? It was the only scenario he could imagine. Dud reached over and turned off the lamp.

Three knocked on his door, yelling, "Come on, Dud, I just saw you turn off the lights." Dud opened up, just a crack.

"Can I come in?" said Three. "What stinks?"

"Earlier I was cooking some exotic cuisine," said Dud. "You're probably picking up on the unusual spices."

"Are you going to let me in?"

"I'm not prepared for visitations. I'm busy working on my novel about the tragic suicides of famous people."

"Well, just put on some pants and come on out, then. I swore to Farrah I'd take you with me on this fucking stakeout, okay? Look, I'll put an extra two hundred in the kitty next week, how does that grab you?"

Dud squeezed out and shut the door quickly behind him. "These *are* my pants, by the way," he said. "The official short hiking pants of a Scoutmaster."

Three laughed. "You're no fucking Scoutmaster," he said.

"No, I happened to buy these at an estate sale, during a visit my late wife and I made to the Bluegrass State, Kentucky, shortly before her demise."

"Well, they look good on you," said Three. "Do you mind if I smoke part of a joint before we get started?" He leaned on one of the two white plaster pillars that seemed to support Dud's sagging porch. It fell over and rolled into the yard, and Three nearly fell with it. When he straightened himself, his downy yellow bangs were hanging in his eyes.

"Whoa!" he said.

"Don't worry, that hasn't been attached in years," said Dud. "I backed the car into it. For reasons that are too complicated to relate, it was my late wife's fault."

"Maybe I should save this for later, huh? A reward for a job well done." Three carefully wrapped his joint in a piece of tinfoil and restored it to the inner pocket of his light linen jacket. "I've got all my life to smoke this joint. So let's make it happen. We're taking your car."

"Why don't we take your car? It's much nicer."

"Exactly. Somebody's bound to notice a sweet fucking ride like that, am I right? We need a piece of crap that won't attract attention."

"I hasten to state that my rather decrepit Escort will certainly attract attention, albeit in an obverse way," said Dud.

"I have no fucking idea what you just said."

"Anyway, a car like yours would be equipped with GPS, wouldn't it?" said Dud. "That would come in handy in a following situation."

"Hey, why don't you be the goon and I'll be the detective? Let's go, let's go." Three snapped his fingers.

"I don't have my keys," said Dud. "They're inside."

"Well, let's go inside and get them. We're on a fucking schedule, laddie."

"Why don't you wait out here and I'll go get them?"

"I need to tinkle," said Three.

"I'd prefer you to do your business outside while I get the keys," said Dud.

"Oh well," said Three. He opened the door and went in ahead of Dud,

tripping over some of the collectibles on the floor. "It's as dark as a fucking tomb in here," he said.

"I live artistically. Sometimes people find it unconventional."

"Where's the toilet? Or let me guess. You pee in a Maxwell House can and leave it in the corner. Is that the way the artists do it? Jesus!"

While Three was in the bathroom Dud rummaged around for his car keys and thought about all the things Three was sure to notice, like the squeezed-out toothpaste tube so old that the petrified gunk leaking out of the cracks was gray, and the permanent stains in the toilet, and the hissing roaches that lived behind the mirror, and the black stuff growing along the rim of the air vent, and the basket of rotting pecans in the bathtub.

3

Three gave Dud the whole rundown while they sat in the dark outside the Hank Williams Museum in Georgiana, waiting for the subject to emerge, Three behind the steering wheel because he had insisted upon driving Dud's car.

The subject was a Frenchman, age 32. Thin and given to wheezing. Brown hair, usually oiled. Mustache. Ornithologist. In the USA on a work visa. Distinguishing physical characteristic: a strange concavity in the middle of his chest, like a hole smoothly covered by skin, for he had been born with his heart too far to the left, nearly; in fact, under his arm. His telephone voice was odd; it frequently made people ask if he were crying. Subject believed that some acoustical property, caused by the unfortunate displacement of his heart, contributed in some manner to this aural illusion.

The Frenchman's American fiancée suspected him of messing around, and furthermore of merely using her for a green card.

"I'm not a good person," said Dud.

"What?" said Three.

"I think I'm starting to turn obsessive-compulsive. Every time I pass gas I say, 'I'm not a good person.'"

"Jesus! Crack a window."

"I told you, we can't roll the windows down. You're the one that picked this car! If I roll down the window it won't roll back up. These french fries taste like fish."

"Mine tasted like french fries."

"There's blood in the straw! Look!"

Sure enough, a thin band of red was visible through the grayish transparency of Dud's plastic straw.

"What the fuck happened?"

"This milkshake is too thick. I had to suck on it so hard it made my mouth bleed."

"You could've waited for it to thaw out a little bit."

"There's your Alabama milkshake. Too thick to drink. I read in a travel magazine about a milkshake you can get in the Caribbean. Just the right temperature. Neither too thick nor too flaccid. A delight. And scented with just a touch of tropical coconut. I ought to have known nobody would know how to make a milkshake around this hellhole."

"God, Dud, you are such a pill. I thought this was going to be fun. Some people like their milkshakes thick. Some people think it indicates the use of real ice cream. Some people, I'd say most people, believe that the thicker the milkshake the higher the quality. Most people have the patience to wait for it to fucking thaw!"

"You drank your whole drink and I haven't even drunk anything yet," said Dud.

"God, do you do anything but whine? I had a Coke, okay? If you ordered a Coke you'd been done right now too. Fuck!"

"I believe cursing to be an affectation of the elite."

"What the fuck are you talking about?"

"It's one of my columns for 'Lumberin' Around!'"

"For what the fuck?"

"I knew Farrah never mentioned it to you. It's a column I want to do for the paper, 'Lumberin' Around!' Actually, I'm glad this came up. It gives me an opportunity to pitch you. As I express it in my column, let's see. I point out that in so-called sophisticated films and videos, it is always the poor who use the fuck word constantly, gangsters and thugs and hoodlums and people of various ethnical derelictions and such. Whereas in real life I grew up poor and among ruffians of all varieties, and I found them to be a reticent and indeed a prudish lot."

"What the fuck are you talking about?"

"My father never had any money, but I recall him going over to a table of young men who were engaging in some banter—harmless banter by today's standards—because his wife and his son were in earshot. That would be myself and my mother. These were clean-cut young men who probably attended a private university, from the looks of them. I remarked at the time on the niceness of their sweaters... a precocious predilection! As I put it in the column. I believe the ribaldry involved a young woman bending over and giving one and all a view of her underpants. And their description was so abstract and oblique that to be honest it was only about a year ago that I figured out what they were talking about. One of them said something like 'rat-a-tat-tat' and pointed his fingers like the barrels of two pistols, trying to show the urgency, I believe, with which his eyes had gone to the suddenly visible sliver of the young lady's underpants. You can imagine how delighted his comrades became at the randy recollection of the rowdy ruffian. That's another direct quote. But those young men obeyed my father's wishes for decorum at once, and with respect. They shushed their mouths and shushed them tight. Whereas today one can't wander out of doors without hearing the fuck word at every public location. If a Frankenstein-like doctor were able to revive him—as I postulate happening in 'Lumberin' Around!'—my late father would no doubt have another stroke within five minutes of his resurrection, very like the one that killed him in the first place. My observation is that those using the fuck word are well-to-do whites of the educated class—stockbrokers, professors of sociology, landed gentry, people with cell phones. Using it loudly, and with a casual pride. They've watched so many movies about the poor, they've adopted this street patois. This elite Hollywood idea of a street patois."

"Hey, Dud, get the fucking stick out of your ass, man."

"Ah yes. Well, I suppose that's the reason I haven't succeeded in the publishing world. If I had a filthy mouth like a gutter and included numerous detailed descriptions of disembowelments littered with the most vulgar profanities imaginable I guess then I would be a best-selling author."

"Yeah, uh-huh, that's probably it."

"The day Miss Tina Brown took over the *New Yorker* magazine I knew in my heart that the fuck word would writhe on its pages like a plague of locusts. These editors, they take one look and say, 'Oh, this fellow is from old working-class Alabama stock. He can't possibly use the fuck word enough to meet our quota of fuck words in this modern publishing world. Let's throw his manuscript directly in the trash can and use his return

postage to mail off our water bill.' And then I suppose they have a good laugh at my expense. The Alabama rube!"

"Subject sighted! Subject sighted!"

4

"Gig Young, the guy who created Plastic Man, the actress who drowned in the toilet," said Dud.

"What the fuck are you babbling about?"

"The three persons I just named all have something very specific in common. They killed themselves. But something's bothering me. I can't recall if Spade Cooley was a murder-suicide or merely a murder."

"I've never heard of a single fucking person you're talking about," said Three.

"That'll all change when my novel comes out," said Dud.

The Frenchman had left the city and driven deep into the country, with Dud and Three following. The highway was still a highway, but it had shrunk to two narrow lanes and there were no streetlights, almost no houses. Stands of trees, broken by an occasional field or orchard.

"Did I tell you about the strange mole on my neck?" said Dud.

"Probably."

"It was just on the spot that my collar rubbed against."

"Your collarbone?"

"Why yes. Isn't that peculiar? I never in my life until now realized why they call it a collarbone. It just never occurred to me to consider the derivation. Certainly it is because that bone is located in such a position as one's collar would rub against. I don't know why I never thought of it before. I truly do learn something new every day."

Three grunted.

"Anyway," said Dud, "I suppose my collar just rubbed on this strange mole every day and eventually it fell off from the sheer friction. The mole did. I got it and put it in an envelope and sealed it up. I was going to bring to the doctor for a biopsy. But don't you know I misplaced that envelope. Can't you just imagine when someone finds it one day? They're going to get some kind of surprise. Delightful. Anyway, I don't suppose it was cancer, knock wood, because I'm not dead yet. I don't recall what I wrote on the front of the envelope. Hey, you passed him!"

The Frenchman had turned and Three had kept going down the highway.

"Of course I passed him," said Three. "We've been the only car behind him for at least thirty minutes. If he's not suspicious yet, he will be if he sees us following him down that red dirt road. We need some tactical distance."

It was a while before they found a place to turn around. When they got back to the dirt road they saw the broken gate at its entrance, the rusty, buckshot-riddled NO TRESPASSING sign. Three switched off the headlights and started down the road, which was wide enough to accommodate no more than one car.

It had rained a few days before, and huge ruts had dried everywhere. The Escort's shocks made the ride even rougher. Dud bit his tongue, clashed his teeth, hit his head on the roof of the car.

"I hate to do this," Three said. He switched on the headlights. "I'm a fucking shitty detective."

Something with flashing yellow eyes ran out in front of the car and bounded into the thicket.

"That GPS sure would come in handy about now."

"How, Dud? How the fuck would it? We don't know where the fuck we're *going*."

Dud shrugged. "I'm just saying," he said.

"I'm cracking this fucking window," said Three.

"Don't you dare!" said Dud.

Three cracked the window and made a big show of gasping for air. "God, it stinks worse out there than it does in here," he said.

"Alabama. Should have thought of that before you rolled down the window," said Dud. "Now it'll never go back up."

"Bullshit." Three tried to roll up the window, but was unsuccessful.

Twenty minutes later they reached the end of the road, and there was literally nothing there. The crickets, locusts, and tree frogs were deafening.

"Huh," said Three. "Where the fuck did he go?"

"He vanished," said Dud.

"Yeah, that's helpful. Well, maybe there was a turnoff somewhere."

They backtracked, and indeed came upon a crossroad they had missed before.

"Which way do we go?" said Dud.

"Well, first we go one way and then we go the other way," said Three.

Taking a right, they almost immediately came to another crossroad.

Three put on the brakes.

"Shit," he said. "I can see I'm going to need some inspiration."

He lit his joint and began to smoke it. Once he held it out for Dud, who declined. "Suit yourself, hotshot," said Three. The car filled with moths, horseflies, gnats, junebugs. Three sat there and smoked his joint until it was nothing but a wet little dot that hardly existed.

After that they drove for a long time, over roads of dirt, roads of oyster shell, roads of gravel, turning whenever Three got a hunch, until they ended up on a road almost too narrow for the Escort, where shrubs and stickers clawed at the doors, branches came in the window and scratched Three's face, and they saw, just up ahead of them, the Frenchman's car parked next to a stream that intersected the path. Three snapped off the lights at once and stopped the car.

"Shit," he said softly.

"Do you think he saw us?"

"I don't the fuck know, Dud. I don't even know where he is."

"It's a good thing his car was there. We could have driven right into that stream."

"I have to admit I'm kind of fucking scared," said Three in a whisper. "Maybe it's the pot."

"Maybe he's sitting up there in that dark car just waiting for us with a tire iron," said Dud.

"Stop making me paranoid. Come on, let's investigate. That's what we're here for, right? There's nothing to be scared of. I have a flashlight with me that costs four hundred dollars. I bet you anything he headed downstream. That's what people do. Go with the flow." Three paused, as if stunned. "Wow. I just realized that's where that expression comes from. I am so stoned!"

"I need you to get out of the car, please. It's going to take me about forty minutes to get your window rolled up. In fact, why don't you go without me? You probably don't want to waste any time, and you have your special flashlight..."

"Leave the window down and let's go. You're my *goon.* This is your time to *shine,* brother, when fucking danger strikes."

"I just don't feel right leaving the window down."

"Do you see where we are? Who do you think's going to want into your shitty car anyway? Count Fucking Dracula?"

"A snapping turtle, a bat, a rabid raccoon or possum, a mosquito carrying the West Nile virus… Look at all the bugs that are already in here."

"How the fuck is a fucking *turtle* going to climb in through the window? Use your fucking noodle, man."

5

They came upon the Frenchman in a clearing defined by a circle of huge, scabby old oaks. He was alone, dressed in something like a beekeeper's outfit. He seemed startled to see them, but only momentarily, then he sprinted toward them, waving his hands.

"The light! The light!"

When he reached them, he tried to force the flashlight from Three's hand. Three struggled. The Frenchman desisted.

"I am sorry," he said. "Must turn off. We use this for light?"

He brought out an iPod, its glowing screen paused on "I Think I Love You," by the Partridge Family.

"I am sorry," said the Frenchman. "You har the honers?"

Three looked at Dud, then back at the Frenchman. "Yes," he said, "we're the honers."

"I do not think you will be… 'ear, you know? I think I can come, it is late, I will bother nobody? I make a study of the birds, you know? Birds?"

"I know birds," said Three.

"I am unting the howl, yes? Not to unt bang-bang. To study. Take picture. You see 'ow I am dress? The bird see me, he think… 'Ah! A tree!'"

The Frenchman seemed to wait for a response from Dud and Three, who were not forthcoming.

"It is good you 'ave appear. You can be my hinformant. 'Ave you 'ear of a howl that glow? A phosphorescent howl?"

"A phosphorescent howl," said Three. "This guy's nuttier than you," he said to Dud.

The Frenchman concentrated on his pronunciation. "Owell," he said.

"Oh! Owl. They don't glow, pal. Sorry to bust your fucking bubble."

"Yes! They do not glow. But some howl do. They 'ave been sightings, you know? People look," (here the Frenchman made binoculars of his hands to illustrate) "and see the phosphorescent howl." He applauded and jumped up and down, pretending to be a person who had just sighted a phosphorescent owl. "But it is, er, undocument? Could be, for me, an himportant discovery. I am thinking it is something the howls eat, per-'ap a glow*worm* or fire*fly*, or possi*bly* a kind of mush*room*. Or could be a moss that get catched in their feather? Or the phosphorescent dung of a certain rare beetle. These are my hypothezee."

"Well, I take it you're not banging somebody out here," said Three. "Not in that outfit. Where's the zipper?"

"I do not bang the howl... bang-bang! No, very careful. Very science."

"Right. Well, knock yourself out, Monsieur Valentin."

"'Ow you know my name?"

"A little howl told me," said Three.

6

They got back on the road home.

"God, I'm the shittiest detective in the world. My cover is totally blown. I'm going to have to call the monsignor and... Did that guy seem gay to you?" said Three.

"It was hard to see him," said Dud.

"Are you listening to me? Goddamnit, I've just solved the fucking case! That guy doesn't have a fiancée. He's too fucking gay. Check it out. That lady was probably a rival scientist, or an imposter *hired* by a rival scientist. I probably did the monsignor a favor. He shouldn't be mixed up with that heartless bitch. Did you see *Chinatown?*"

"Where are we? Is this the right way?"

"I don't the fuck know, Dud. Why couldn't he have driven north to Lumber Land instead of south to Bumfuck? Did you see *Chinatown?*"

"I saw it on the big screen at its inception," said Dud. "To this day I have no idea what the grand folderol was about."

"Are you fucking kidding me? It's classic. My sister! My daughter! My sister! My daughter!"

"Have you ever had the problem of phosphorescent urine?" asked Dud.

"Can't say that I have."

"Do you think it's common? The owls made me think of it. Several nights ago I was urinating with the light off and I noticed that my urine had a faint white phosphorescence to it."

"That could come in handy. Now could you please shut the fuck up for two minutes so maybe I could figure out where the fuck we are?"

Dud was silent for a spell and then he made a little grunt like he had thought of something private and fascinating.

"What?"

"Huh? Oh!" Dud pretended to be surprised that Three had heard his meaningful grunt. "Oh, nothing. I was just thinking about how many great novels I could have written."

"How many?"

"Fourteen."

"Wow."

"And I'm not talking about these little skinny novels everybody writes nowadays. I refuse to read any novel that's under 800 pages long."

"Hey, you're deep," said Three.

"Trouble is, I can't write any of my novels until everybody I know is dead. I wrote a great one about my dead wife but I had to dispose of it out of guilt feelings. I really shouldn't blame her, but I do."

"On a personal note?" said Three. "It makes me uncomfortable that you blame everything on your dead wife. I think the word I'm looking for is *un-fucking-gentlemanly*."

"That's easy for you to say. You don't have a dead wife."

"Did you have fun tonight?" said Three.

"Fun? What's fun? I haven't had fun in so long I don't even know what fun is."

"Did you find it pleasant being a detective's goon? Is it something you could see yourself doing in the future? Think about it. It would give you plenty of material for your writing career."

"I already have too much material. It paralyzes me as a writer. I wish I didn't have so many brilliant ideas! It's my tragic flaw. All the ideas try to get out and they jam together in my brain, causing mental stagnation."

"What I'm trying to say is, if anything like this comes up again I'll be able to use you. But you can't come around the railroad car anymore. You bother Farrah."

"Well, I highly doubt that. She appears to enjoy our little conversations."

"Yeah, well, let's just say she enjoys them so much you distract her from her work. The railroad car is off-limits, man."

"What about my assignments?" said Dud. "How will I get my newspaper assignments?"

"When's the last time you had an assignment, buddy? Never?"

"Yes, technically never, I guess," said Dud.

"That's right. Look, it was in the old man's will for you to be on retainer. You're like a family project or something, ever since Granddad tried to send you to manage that rubber plantation."

"But I had a case of hysterical dysentery on the ocean liner. That is, I *thought* I was going to have dysentery at any moment, so they let me off. It's just as bad as real dysentery in its way."

"Have you noticed how my family has a propitiatory fucking tenderness about your ass? I don't know. Maybe you're my illegitimate uncle or some shit nobody bothered to tell me. But there's no reason for you to keep coming down and bothering Farrah. She just cuts and pastes stuff off the internet, that's the whole newspaper, it doesn't take a team of fucking muckrakers. And trust me, you bother her. She asked me to speak to you about this."

"May I make the suggestion that you pay me all the money at once?"

"All what money?"

"However much money you think you will pay me on this *retainer* before I die."

"When are you planning on dying, Dud?"

"In about forty years, I suppose."

"Well, that's a lot of money to pay at once."

"Yes, but it would be off your mind and I could open the sophisticated restaurant I've always dreamed of. Have I ever told you about my restaurant?"

"I'm sure you have."

"Can you describe it for me, then?"

Three gritted his teeth.

"Let me refresh your memory, assuming for the moment that it is somewhere *in* your memory, which I highly doubt because I don't believe I've mentioned this to a living soul. I used to tell my late wife about it and she found the whole idea reckless. I explained to her that owning a restaurant would free me up for the leisure time I needed to contemplate my writing activities. Of course she refused to acquiesce. Maybe you could just be a backer, an investor. It's called Amburger. No, don't say anything, let me describe it. All I'm going to serve is variations on the common hamburger. The signature burger, the 'Amburger,' is just that—a classic, simple hamburger. The Bamburger will be designed by Emeril LaGasse, a famous chef who says 'Bam!' a lot. The Camburger will be a cheeseburger topped with Camembert cheese. The Damburger will have a piquant dash of Tabasco— 'dam' being a subtle play on the idea of damnation and hellfire. The Edamburger, and yes, you might say I'm cheating on this one a bit, phonetically speaking…"

"Are there, like, twenty-six of these?"

"The Edamburger will of course be topped with Edam cheese. The Famburger is merely a plain bun served with a side of water. I don't expect anyone to order that one. It refers to famine, of course, and may be considered a symbolic nod to political consciousness or compassionate conservatism, as I like to call it. The Gamburger is made with the meat of a chicken leg, 'gam' being old-time movie slang for a leg, particularly the leg of a gorgeous woman. My Hamburger, contrary to expectation, comes with a slice of the finest Virginia ham. The I Am Burger is made to order at the customer's personal specifications, and can include any ingredient on the menu in any combination. Or I may make it the Iamburger instead, one word, a burger with exactly five ingredients, referring to the five beats in a line of iambic pentameter, although that may be asking too much of the customer, which is why I'm leaning toward the former interpretation. The Jamburger utilizes homemade red pepper jelly from my deceased wife's recipe."

"Jesus Christ! Can you shut the fuck up?" Three had screamed so loudly, and with so much fervor and sincerity, that his voice seemed to shatter, and giant globes of spit hit the steering wheel and the windshield and lingered on his chin.

Dud was silent for about ninety seconds. Then he gasped and cried out: "Oh, my taint!"

"What now?"

Tears were rolling out of Dud's eyes. "Something stung me on the taint," he said. "It's paralyzed! Something has paralyzed my poor taint, do you comprehend me? Oh God, stop the car."

"You are so full of it. What's a fucking taint?"

"It's the area between my scrotum and…"

"Thanks for sharing," Three sang in a weird, girlish voice, as if it were a phrase and an affectation that Dud should recognize.

Dud felt a thousand splinters all around his private area. It was different from his usual ailments, like the difference between dreaming and waking.

"So this is what it's like," he said.

"What what the fuck is like?" said Three.

"Dying," said Dud, and he let out a terrible cry.

"Are you about done?" said Three.

"Where is it? Where did it go? Save yourself!" said Dud. He was trying to get out of his Scoutmaster pants.

"Ouch!" said Three. "Oh fuck! Oh shit! Snake!"

Three pulled off the road in a hurry. He and Dud jumped out, moaning and hollering. The doors of the car were flung wide, the lights were on, the Escort kept going until it hit a tree, but Dud and Three were out, stumbling and falling, Dud into the briars and Three into the road.

"I was bitten first," said Dud. "Will you extract the venom from my taint?"

"Are you fucking…" said Three, but could not finish his thought. He flopped in the road like a hurt bird. His hand was at his neck and blood was squirting through his fingers.

Dud tried to crawl toward Three but he couldn't feel his legs. He dug his hands into the thorny brush and pulled himself toward the road, dragging his useless bottom half behind him. The hot, needling pain had traveled up his back and into his shoulders and arms but he kept pulling. A searing nausea hit him in waves, whiting out the shape of Three, which twisted and jerked in clouds of dust. As he pulled himself across the wilderness, Dud shook his head to clear it again and again. When he reached Three, Dud gathered his poor strength and raised himself up. He cradled Three's head and upper body in his lap and prepared to suck.

"Look at me, God!" Dud said aloud to the woods. "Look at me, world! I'm rising to the crisis! I'm rising to the crisis! I'm rising to the crisis! I'm rising to the crisis!" Then he looked down at Three, whose mouth and throat had apparently frozen up in a horrible way. Something white was coming out. He was making a sound that sounded something like *Fuck*. He seemed to die.

"Great," said Dud to Three. "Thanks for nothing."

Dud lay Three's dead body on the ground. He got down beside Three and positioned his mouth on the gory throat, as if he had been selflessly sucking the poison despite his own grave wounds that were killing him as well.

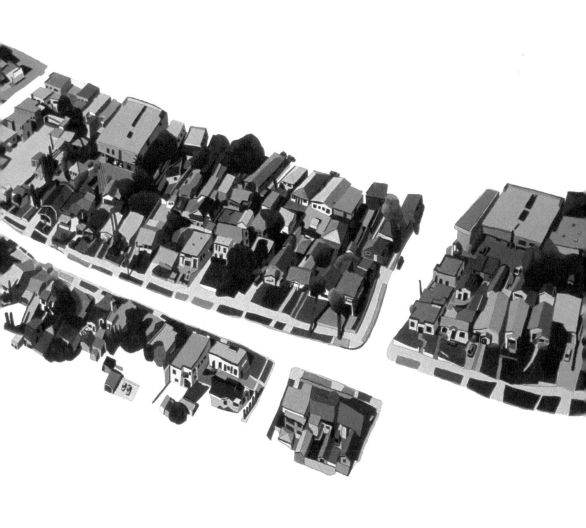

I wish I could see what this looks like, he thought.

There came a sound like rushing wind and suddenly he was floating over the scene, which turned out to be just the way he had pictured it.

"Yes," said Dud. "Perfect."

LOESS

by ROY KESEY

—A FEW QUESTIONS first, if I may.

    —And of course.

    —Fine, then. The goal?

    —There are two: the overthrow of this world, and the construction of the next.

    —Right. And what, may I ask, are your qualifications?

    —I have read the classics, farmed rice, kept accounting records. I was a soldier for six months. I applied and was accepted to police school, law school, and soap-making school but did not attend. I went to business school for a month. There were other schools as well. Then I became a librarian's assistant. During winter holidays I walked through the country-side, and took rain-baths when it rained. Also I have edited newspapers and organized certain organizations.

    —Outstanding.

    —Are you with me, then?

    —Entirely. Will we work together or in parallel?

    —In parallel for now, and later together. For now you shall go and I shall stay, and in our respective places we shall organize still more

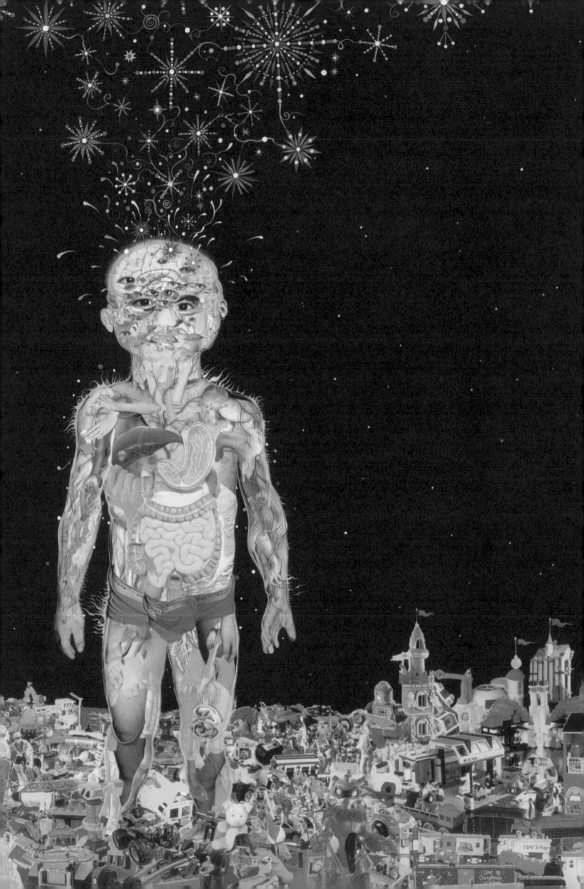

organizations. Then you will return, and we will ally with our domestic enemy against the foreign invaders; I will help to plan uprisings for you and others to lead, and they will be wildly successful and then fail horribly as the alliance dissolves. You will be captured by our domestic enemy, and your execution order will be signed, and a former student of yours will help you escape; I will also be captured, and my execution order will also be signed, and I too will escape, and hide in tall grass until nightfall, and slip away. Nearly all of the members of our organizations shall subsequently and quickly be slaughtered. Is that all right with you?

—Perfectly. To work.

It was not simple, but it was managed, that which has been mentioned, and other things: a flag was raised, and an army. Thought was remolded forcibly when necessary, and of course the domestic enemy began extermination campaigns. The foreign invaders took the northeast, and in the northwest there was famine, men and boys standing beside roads, their stomachs swollen with dirt and bark and sawdust, men and boys only as the women and girls had already died or been sold; men and boys standing naked having exchanged all possessions even clothing for food and they stood and the sun weighted their skin and they stood and their eyes closed and still they stood and then died: several million.

Extermination Campaigns One through Four were turned back, the defenders successfully melding elasticity and mobility, secrecy and ambush. During the Fifth Campaign, however, these requisites were mislaid; the domestic enemy routed and chased them, and executed their families, and likewise killed or else relocated all others who lived in areas under dispute, the short-haired and/or large-footed women all killed, and the long-haired, small-footed women made concubines, and the children called war orphans and sent as slaves or prostitutes to cities, and when a million more were dead it was time for another plan.

—We cannot stay here any longer.
  —And where will we go?
  —North, to the cradle.

—But our domestic enemy lies wholly between it and us.

—So we shall travel circuitously: six thousand miles of walking and fighting, walking and fighting.

—But most of us are shoeless!

—Unfortunately yes.

—Through twelve provinces…

—And over eighteen mountain ranges, and across twenty-four rivers.

—Walking and fighting and climbing and crossing without rest?

—Of three hundred and sixty-eight days we shall spend two hundred and fifty marching; we shall skirmish daily, and fight fifteen major battles, but otherwise, yes, rest, though even that rest will be not rest but sharing, speaking with those through whose lands we walk and fight, and we shall need a way to convince them not only to join us but to lose their very them-ness and subsist in all five senses of the word in us-ness, not one-of-us-ness but us-ness itself…

—Perhaps… Perhaps theater!

—Theater! With messages!

—Anti-foreign-invaders-and-domestic-enemies, for example.

—And pro-us.

—Superb, but we precede ourselves. The four lines of domestic enemy defensive works, their nine regiments, how will we—

—Walking and fighting, walking and fighting. We shall march at night when possible; the wounded will be left behind with those few who can be spared to fight rearguard, two years or three, as long as they last, and any leaders caught then paraded naked in bamboo cages and beheaded. Once through, a feint south, then a push west to the first of the rivers, a doubling-back, a ploy, a quick battle, and we'll all be across in nine days.

—What then of the Lolos?

—We shall ally with them, and follow them on and through to the Tatu. The river will rise and swell and rage as we ferry our army across on three boats left stupidly unburned, constant aerial strafing as of the third morning and the domestic enemy pushing hard towards us and no choice then for those not yet across but west to the Bridge Fixed by Liu.

—Liu!

—Liu. Those already crossed shall fight and we shall race but the domestic enemy will arrive first, will remove all planking from our half of the bridge, will emplace machine guns.

—And then?

—The chains. Volunteers, hand over hand, and they shall mainly be annihilated, but one shall make it halfway across, shall then hang beneath and be protected by unremoved planking, shall throw grenades and shout terms of encouragement, the bridge will be ordered burned but too late, those already crossed will arrive and the enemy will run.

—That is fortunate.

—Very.

—Then the highlands and mountains.

—Yes, and here many more shall be lost to the cold, the fatigue, the precipices. But there will also be things worth taking from those with too much: ham and duck and salt.

—Duck!

—Precisely.

—But what of the Hsifan, and the tribal Mantzu?

—They shall roll boulders upon us, and we in turn shall steal and eat their wheat, their beets, their massive turnips. Many too will be lost to the swamps, and there will be no shelter from the rain, and there will be no fire to cook our food or warm our bodies, but the cradle will at last not be so distant.

—And having once arrived—

—After several more battles here undescribed—

—Where exactly will we live?

—In the caves.

—Cave-caves?

—Loess caves!

—Loess, of course, loess. But will there be enough of them?

—We shall not need so many by then.

—Heavy losses?

—Eighty percent.

—Disastrous.

—Disastrous indeed, but survivable.

It was not simple, but it was managed, that which has been mentioned, and other things. The caves were temperate and dry, and soon were fitted with floors of stone, rice-paper windows, and lacquered doors. The lower loess slopes fluted down toward fields of wheat, corn, millet; the hills themselves

were twisted and scored by water and wind, and with the changing of the light became brigantines, ballrooms, battlements.

New preparations, then, and new organizations: the Young Vanguards, the Children's Brigades, the Elder Brother Society. Large-footed women cleared and planted; small-footed women pulled weeds and collected dung. And of course all that was owned by those who owned much was taken: goods, crops, land.

Old poisons were drained, and all doors replaced when soldiers left homes they had been lent. Mass justice took the form of executions. Factories were looted for necessary machinery; handbills dropped by the enemy giving bounty amounts for each leader were flipped and bound for schoolbooks.

The question, now, was time and how to fill it. Responses: classes on reading and writing, and political lectures, each student bringing his or her brick to answer the lack of chairs. There were public health and factory efficiency competitions. Clay models served as instructional aids for history and geography, strategy and tactics, anatomy and surgery. There were broadsheets giving praise, criticism, and something a little like news. There was ping-pong. When military circumstances permitted there were group walks into the hills, gazelles and buzzards to watch, and hot water was drunk, and it was called white tea. There were card games, war songs sung to the music of old hymns, and of course always theater, needed greatly now as policies occasionally changed: in the first act of each play the old policies were followed and errors were thus committed and hundreds died theatrically; in the second act the new policies were followed and the result was invariably triumphant marching.

Throughout all this there were constant small fruitless attacks on their base, but then the domestic enemy erred: its leader was captured in transit while organizing Extermination Campaign Number Six. He capitulated immediately, and all agreed that the foreign invaders might at last be engaged and dislodged from their positions in the northeast.

The invaders however did not wait for them to arrive; instead they schemed at the Marco Polo Bridge and came in full, took half of the country but were attacked on all fronts and driven far though hardly out. Soon on other continents too there were millions on ships and in tanks and on foot dying, and the war here against the foreign invaders became part of that greater war, a war that took all the world; this greater war ended well, the invaders driven now wholly out, new bombs dropped by greater allies, the no-longer-invaders disappearing in smoke, their shadows burned into their concrete.

—And now?

—Another war.

—The domestic enemy again, yes. Will they be definitively defeated?

—It will take three years, but in the end the remnants will be driven to an island, and the remnants will pretend to be us, but they will not be us, and the world will be made to know.

—Peace, then.

—Yes.

—Stability at last.

—Also.

—The world overthrown, you and I together as before, all else below us and time for a construction of the new.

—Though for a project of that nature and size, perhaps we would do well to invite the participation of others.

—Others, yes, to make manifest that which we design. A Minister of Commerce! of Education! of Industry!

—These yes of course, but more importantly, no fewer than four hagiographers. Someone to rewrite all literature, and a former emperor to garden. And for our army commander we shall need someone whose grandmother insisted he be drowned for lack of loyalty when as a child he kicked her opium pan from the stove; someone who fled his home at the age of nine, became a cowherd, then worked the bellows in a coal mine for fourteen hours per day; someone who labored without pay as a shoemaker's apprentice, then in a sodium mine which soon closed; someone who also has worked as a dike builder, who in two years saved a total of twelve dollars immediately rendered worthless upon a change of warlords and thus currencies; someone who has led starving farmers to sack the rice bins of the rich and the not-rich-but-also-not-poor, who became a soldier, attempted to assassinate a governor and failed but escaped, became a spy, was captured and tortured an hour a day for a month, confessed nothing and was released, attended officer school, rose through ranks, led insurrections and founded local governments and accompanied us on our long walk.

—I believe that I know such a man.

—Wonderful! But…

—Yes?

—Beyond the peace I cannot see. It is as if—

—I can.

—Can what?

—See beyond.

—But how?

—The gift has been given.

—And? How will it go?

—You shall begin well, abolishing the sales tax, the camel tax, the salt carrying tax, the salt consumption tax, and also the taxes on pigeons, middlemen, land, food, special food, additional land, coal, pelts, tobacco, wine, stamps, boats, irrigation, millstones, houses, wood, milling, marriage, and vegetables.

—Magnificent!

—But you will also have certain other ideas.

—Will they too provoke happiness?

—Those with differing ideas will be accused of mistakes of subjectivism, of economism, of reactionary and feudalistic atavisms; you will order them killed or imprisoned.

—Yes, but my ideas, will they provoke happiness?

—You will have the entire country making steel in their backyards.

—Steel is important!

—All other work will be abandoned; factories, schools, and hospitals will close, and the crops shall rot in the fields.

—Oh.

—In the following years, unfortunate droughts shall occur.

—Ah.

—Perhaps forty million will die.

—That is a large number.

—Immense, yes.

—We have many to spare, however.

—Spare?

—And we can always tell everyone that it was nonetheless a success.

—That is an option, yes.

—And then?

—Your power shall be reduced, and things shall be returned to how they were before your steel idea insofar as that is possible.

—Unthinkable!

—Yes, and nonetheless true, but you will subsequently recover much of the power you had lost.

—Excellent.

—Well...

—What?

—You shall stage your own foreign invasion of a nearby land filled with glaciers and temples and yaks so as to secure hydrological resources in perpetuity, infuriating actors and actresses everywhere. And you shall apply all your remaining energy to designing and implementing a new system of primary education; soon enough the children will be very young adults who will praise you and act vastly in your name.

—They will perform great feats?

—Feats, at any rate. They shall worship you, shall announce that all you say is true. You will disappear, then return, and employ them to destroy all who oppose you.

—That sounds all right.

—In a manner of speaking. Unfortunately you shall have additional ideas.

It was not simple, but it was managed, that which has been mentioned. Also, other things. A play satirizing their leadership gave the necessary opening; gambits were played, counterattacks organized, tentacles extended.

The result: eleven million teenagers now held all practical power. Playing hooky pleased them, as did the establishment of tribunals and the meting out of punishment. Intellectuals were of course pilloried first. When there were no more intellectuals the teenagers went simply from house to house, even into their own houses, and brought their families forth. The chewing of broken glass was obligatory in certain circumstances, and of course millions died.

All who might at some point provide opposition were reeducated in labor camps. Classical musicians were made to play outdoors in the rain to keep sparrows from landing on branches; economists were made to catch cockroaches, and to count them; and all were made to make bricks, and paint asphalt streets, and dig large holes.

The teenagers smiled at the police and the army and bade them crawl. They set fire to libraries and museums, temples and mosques and churches. Any who did not now participate or cheerlead were likewise pilloried, or sent to the provinces to shovel manure, or obliged to write about the wrong things they liked, such as Mozart, that they might better be criticized for liking wrongly.

—That was unfortunate.

　—Yes, and it is not yet quite finished.

　—Is there to be a future upside?

　—You shall continue to be praised as a god for a time.

　—All right then.

　—Though in fact by this point you shall be only a figurehead.

　—And who will hold true control? You?

　—No. Others. I shall try only to slow the worst of them. And my power too shall fade. A coup will be attempted, but you will escape, will still have certain allies, and the coup leaders will be caught and disappeared. Later, other rivals will emerge; by then you will be mainly insensate in all three senses of the word, and I shall just barely defeat them, and the worst of it shall be over.

　—And we rise again?

　—No, we die. Me first, then you.

　—But afterwards our works live on?

　—For a time. Then they are repudiated. Then they are ignored. Then they are forgotten.

　—Will we at least be remembered?

　—Your body shall be preserved, though not much later everyone will wonder why. Our names, of course, our names will be remembered. Hundreds of millions of copies of your sayings will have been sold but will now be seldom read.

　—And who will then lead?

　—The man who shall establish the Two Whatevers.

　—These whatevers, they will be successful?

　—No. And he who established them shall not last long; curiously, the next man to lead will be one whom we regularly demoted and often discussed eradicating but never quite did.

—Will he lead well?

—In some respects, considering. He shall rehabilitate many in need, though nearly all those who thought will be gone irrevocably. After him there will be others, and the same shall be said of them. By then your sayings will be tourist curiosities. All policies will head in directions other than that in which we led. Those who destroyed in your name will be tried and imprisoned and executed where practicable. Your mistakes will continue to be condemned. Martial law will be applied at times, and new protestors suppressed—in this at least things shall be consistent.

—I had hoped for better.

—I know.

—Ah, well.

—Indeed. There is always the further future, of course, though it cannot yet be seen.

—Onward, then.

—Onward, yes, onward.

HOUSES FOR FISHES

by ANTHONY SCHNEIDER

WHILE WE WERE talking, I switched on the television and imagined that your words were being spoken by the woman in the sitcom and, when she was not in the scene, by one of the men who remained. After a while, I looked at you again, frowning so that you wouldn't discern my motive. Your lips were out of sync like a dubbed movie, but it was easy to believe the babble of conversation and canned laughter emanated from your mouth.

I spent the better part of a morning looking at the world through a web of fingers, one eye shut, the other eye pressed close to the square gap between perpendicular digits. A lampshade filled my contrived screen, and only an edge of the kitchen sink was visible, a pleasingly curved white orb between fuzzy fleshy borders.

Another time, I squinted, eyes open just a crack, until the room became a blur, the chair almost indecipherable from the bookcase behind it, the door handle no more than a gray smudge in a field of white, and when you stood up you looked like a tree seen from afar, in mist or fog perhaps.

Do you remember when I was reading that book and you spoke to me, and I answered quite conversationally but with words cribbed from the novel in my hands? You just shook your head and asked, Who are you being? thinking I was imitating some new comedian or actor. Scholsdorff, I answered with a name on the page, but if you understood you gave no indication.

We were watching an old movie. I lowered the volume on the television and raised the volume on the radio. On the screen, a star-crossed couple was having a conversation in a city park. But there was only one voice, an irascible talk radio caller spouting racial epithets and blaming unemployment on Hispanics and the new mayor.

I set the table all wrong, laid celery instead of forks, pencils instead of knives, CD jewel-cases where the napkins usually went. You picked up the not-cutlery and put it in a bowl. You said it wasn't funny. You said you were tired.

I replaced the map in your car with one of another city, slid advertisements from the newspaper into the picture frames in our living room, switched the covers of books. I bought uncut keys at the hardware store and put them on your key ring. I poured flour into the sugar bowl, yeast into the bag of flour, scooped mustard into the peanut butter jar, replaced the milk with orange juice. And set all the clocks for a distant time zone.

While you were sleeping, I changed into a brand new pair of pants and a shirt I'd worn only once. My suitcase was waiting in the hallway, and I left the apartment without making a sound.

ELSEWHERE

by RODERICK WHITE

YOU DIE AND go to heaven. Heaven is a long, white hallway with many rooms. The Baptists are in one room, the Jews in another. It's a long hallway. At the very end are the Mormons. "You must be quiet with passing this door," they tell you when you arrive, "because the Mormons think they're the only ones here."

Derek Taylor, the first poet to die, grew up in Ogden, Utah, and like many people from this state had shiny blond hair and blue eyes.

"Light flows from you," his best poem begins. "You are another nature."

He had been sent home from his church mission in Australia the previous spring when one of his host sisters (there were three beautiful teenage daughters) opened the bathroom door and discovered Derek with a handful of Vaseline. This was the first thought that came to my mind that night—that at least Derek would be remembered for something else—when I watched the park rangers live on the local news pull his limp, floating body feet-first out of the Great Salt Lake amidst a blizzard of shrieking seagulls.

Earlier that same evening Sara Whitaker, another student in the graduate program, shot her hand up after David Roper, our teacher, the Poet Laureate of the United States, scrawled on the blackboard in neat, block letters, "I fucked your mother last night." Turning to the class, he smelled his long, stiff fingers like a very tall pitcher sniffing a mitt.

"Go home, Dad," answered Sara behind a veil of uncombed, golden hair. "You're drunk."

It was our favorite game—advancing improbable first lines.

Less than a month later two joggers found Sara's body nude hanging like a witch in a cluster of yellow, clicking trees near Temple Square.

"A wonder lasts nine days," Roper read aloud at the funeral before crying out and collapsing, requiring four men to carry him.

In an editorial in the *Tribune* the two deaths are linked cynically to Sylvia Plath, the only mention of poetry I'd ever seen in the paper other than the occasional citing of Professor Roper receiving another award. Privately, there is talk of more sinister goings-on; namely, drugs and the emergence of Satan in the valley. Counselors, then police, are quietly made available to us.

Cupping my lucky seashell against my ear and listening to the echo of the ocean far away, I rest my head on my desk in the back of the library and close my eyes, not opening them until the clock strikes midnight when the beautiful librarian rises silently from behind her large desk and to my utter horror takes the arm of Alex Field, yet another Arian poet in the program, the rumored heir to the Mrs. Field's cookie empire, flicking the switch off as she leaves.

Where We Are Now

I wrote a haiku before erasing the whole damn thing—

In a parking lot
With just a grocery bag
Of apples, in June.

*   *   *

Waking in the same bed my mother dreamed in as a child, I realize only now that no one within a thousand miles in any direction knows that it is my twenty-fourth birthday. I spit my night-guard into the sink and soak in the tub until my fingers and the like shrivel. I am becoming like a sad, sad sperm whale, I tell myself. How, I wonder, beached in cold, soapy foam, my feet a fluke, do I find another like me?

I fry bacon while flipping through the newspaper, my eye catching finally on a short paragraph near the bottom of page sixteen. "Elsewhere," the headline reads. Recently a homeless man had been arrested beneath the Kremlin, the story begins, after allegedly discovering Peter the Great's legendary library of golden books. He had opened an unlocked door, the man claimed, in some overgrown public garden, soon finding himself inside a narrow tunnel that led to a room where the great books shined. Regrettably, a government official explained, the man had been drinking. Now no one is sure of the exact location of the door, or even if it had been in a garden at all. I start reading the story over again, my bacon burning, when an envelope slides under my door.

I open the door amuck in my underwear but find no one. The empty hallway gapes. I hold the envelope close to my eyes. How could this be? I tear it open and to my astonishment it is a birthday card: a cartoon of a man and women looking up into the night sky. On the inside is the unsigned, printed inscription: *If a constellation were named after you, it would be phallic and largely insignificant.*

"It's probably not related," says Detective Kohl on the phone. Then he asks if anyone in my life has any reason to be vindictive.

"I haven't gotten laid since I moved out here," I tell him. "Not even close."

"Lower your voice, sir."

"Shouldn't I be concerned about this?"

"It just takes a little bit longer with Utah girls," he says.

Beer bars close early in Utah. The social clubs (bars that serve liquor) stay open later, but the yearly dues are too much for us. Sebastian and I walk up the mountain quietly in the snow. Sebastian is a poet, too. He moonlights as a professional wrestler on a local television station. He always loses. "I used to work at Burger King, so relax," he introduced himself loudly at an orientation party before bumping into Alex Field and spilling his drink onto Mr. Field's green cashmere coat. "Please think of me as the spawn of Kit Marlowe and Emily Dickinson," he asked. Was he actually ogling me over the brim of his wine glass? "Has anyone ever told you that you look like F. Scott Fitzgerald?" Sebastian giggled, moonfaced, before eventually passing out in the middle of Professor Roper's lawn. I was one of the last students to leave that night. I too drank more than I should have and lingered too long in Roper's study, wondering how many poems in the *New Yorker* had been written right here. Tucked away in the dark corner of a bookshelf I found a picture of him with Mick Jagger and a very young Madonna taken at Studio 54 or someplace like it.

When I shook his hand goodnight he said to me, "You have the softest hands." He hummed softly to himself. He seemed almost as embarrassed as me, both of us pretending not to hear Sebastian in the bushes retching.

"Do you know how hard it is to steal a giraffe out of the zoo?" asks Sebastian, tightroping the curb now, arms spread like a bird. "First, you have to back it into a trailer. That can take hours. Then—and this is the part I could never figure out—then you have to drive down roads with no overpasses or low wires. Because, you know, you don't want to decapitate it."

I look up at the dirty moon.

"I used to drive for hours looking for ways out of the zoo." He stops dead in his tracks as if remembering something important. "A policeman sent me a note today with a smiley face on it."

"Have you talked to the police?" I ask.

"Not since the last attempt," he says, not at all concerned, his stomach growling from the smell of warm bread. "They took my gun away, but I bought another." He pulls out the plastic revolver loaded with drink from the inside pocket of his raincoat. It glistens in his hand, just as it did a week earlier before class when he casually plopped it down in the center of the table in front of all of us and spun it around without saying a word.

"We ought to break in there one night." He points his size fifteen boot at the bread factory across the street. "Eat a bunch of bread."

"What attempt?"

Sebastian pirouettes off the curb and lands with both boots together, less like Fred Astaire than like a trained bear, aiming the gun at a faded billboard before squirting the nectar into his mouth.

"What attempt are you talking about?" I ask in a trembling voice.

Above us the billboard of a missing child hums.

"The giraffes," he says.

When I get home I find elaborate drawings in blue and red chalk across the driveway of my apartment building. The surface is flat and smooth, a natural canvas, but sometimes I like to think the children choose this spot because I live here.

"Do you like it?" a boy asks, kneeling in the center of the driveway, his hands blue with chalk.

The drawing is large, over eight feet long and as wide as the driveway.

"It's a secret tunnel," he says.

Another child scribbles in purple.

"This is a fountain," she tells me. "Do you know why fountains have pennies?"

"Because people are desperate," I hear myself say.

"No." She turns around to smile at me. "It's because people are cheap."

Sometimes I would find lipstick smudges on the coffee cups my mother used. I would imagine that the smudges were blood, and that I was a detective tracing a murder. I remember seeing those same red smudges the morning my father explained to me that he would not be living with us for a while. "It's nothing you've done," he told me. He fried bacon and eggs; halfway through he turned to me and said, "If you are anything like me the urge to kiss a beautiful, unfamiliar woman will sometimes strike quite urgently. After all," his voice deepened after a gurgle of laughter, "that is how you began." This is one of the ways poems are written.

I keep thinking of Peter Taylor, the writer. The first thing they made us read in college was Taylor's "The Old Forest," a short story set in Memphis in which a young woman disappears after a car accident. At the time I empathized strongly with the narrator/young Southern gentleman in peril. In a way I suppose I had always desired such a life for myself—mysterious women jumping out of cars, the real threat of scandal, danger.

The truth is that I have not been doing very well. My writing has inspired no one within a thousand miles in any direction, not even me. "How hard it is to look into Josephine's mirror and not feel a little like Napoleon," said Professor Roper in class, looking down at me, "and how sad."

In an epic poem yet to be written I wake in the gutter beside my rusted bicycle as the sun rises along my finger. "Potential," shrieks the parrot upon my entering the tropical pet store. "I will not tell you there is nothing to fear," mumbles the old man who shoulders the beast, his face puckered by fire.

Instead of unifying the class, the deaths only heighten our differences. Geography, of all things, has come between us. Sebastian and I are the only two students (he from Ohio) not from the mountain-time zone.

"Paranoia, Watson, is natural in situations like this," says Sebastian, pawing at a slice of pizza in the student center.

"Maybe we should get out of here for a while."

"That would look awfully incriminating now, wouldn't it?" he says. "Other than the occasional mass murder and ritual suicide, what other crimes are there in Utah?" He points his fork. "Ted Bundy, you know, not only went to undergrad here but also law school. Probably sat right here."

We watch the line form for ice cream. Even when it's twenty degrees outside people still stand in line for ice cream.

"Look at it this way," he says. "What about the two years, not to mention thousands of dollars in student loans, that we've invested for a degree that, okay, while virtually useless in today's job market, would nonetheless be kind of cool to have?"

"Doesn't it bother you," I ask, "living like this?"

"Whenever I'm scared I have this little trick," he says matter-of-factly. "I imagine that I'm the young Lawrence of Arabia in white linen dress. My eyes shine bluely. I know I'll be all right then."

We sit silently watching the room fill with Mormons and ex-Mormons

"Let's be honest," he tells me. When he pushes his tray away I see myself twinned in his cool brown eyes. "My poetry has never been better."

* * *

Muse

Armed with only a dictionary
Of superstitions
The beautiful librarian

Leads me by the hand.
"These are yours," she says,
Motioning to many books.

"But to read them means
You'll never write them."
She wears pants that zip

From behind, and though
I'm very young, five or six,
I feel a hard-on coming on.

Amid a myriad of death poems, the midnight sky my backdrop, I move on the librarian. She sits perched again behind the counter in the Rare Books Room, her dark hair tied back tonight in a bun. She has the littlest ears I've ever seen.

"Would you please consider going out with me sometime very soon?" my voice shakes.

Her fierce, olive eyes blink reflexively as if in the beam of a bright light. "You're a poet, aren't you?" she asks.

"Only after erasing most of what I've written."

"The 'very' in 'very soon'—the way you said it when you asked me out—that's why I decided to do this," Karen tells me after she locks her door. "Don't get any funny ideas, though," she says, rolling the key in her sock. "I'm wearing a Wonder Bra."

"I thought we'd go to the zoo," I say. "It's less than a mile."

"I've never been."

"It's a nice, clean zoo. The animals have plenty of room. You can tell a lot about a city from its zoo."

"You're not from here, are you?" She smiles.

"Atlanta."

"Never met anyone from Atlanta before."

"Very few people are actually from Atlanta," I tell her.

We stop at the corner and cross over.

"I'm from St. George," she says. "Ever been to the desert?"

"No."

"It's beautiful. All of Utah is beautiful except for the Great Salt Lake. God's country."

"I was most surprised by the rednecks. They're the same kind that we have in Georgia."

"Even China has rednecks, I bet," she says. "They just call them something else." She walks slightly ahead of me on the sidewalk. Her body really moves.

"Aren't you scared?" I ask all of a sudden.

"Only when I'm alone with a poet."

"Sometimes I feel like I'm in *Platoon*," I joke, "going into the bush with nothing but poetry, but instead of the bush I wake up in the library."

She looks at me closely for the first time, as though idling momentarily at the crest of a steep hill.

"I like to think of libraries as churches in a time of war," she tells me. "Sacred ground where anyone can visit or hide. I was in a wheelchair until I was four," she pauses, stone-faced. "I taught myself how to walk by watching horses on my grandmother's farm. That's why it looks like I'm walking on hind legs."

"No," I say a little too loudly, trying not to look again at her long legs.

"I spent my whole childhood reading. My grandmother used to tell me that my mother was impregnated by a poet who must surely have been a horse in a past life, or a jackass."

Neither of us says anything for a long time as the snow swirls around our faces; then all at once, like a hiccup after a gulp of beer, like the whirr of a broken wing, her laugh is released. It whiffs through the air and tickles my ears. I breathe it into my nose, deep inside the soft, pink lump of my brain, as cold as charity.

"I'm getting over mono," she explains, tilting her head back and exposing her throat like a ballerina's. "Tonsils as big as testicles." She tries not to smile, her green eyes momentarily alighting on mine. "Tell me to shut up."

I close my eyes and imagine that we're inside one of those snow globes with plastic snow and little people. Somebody is shaking it up.

"Do you trust me?" Sebastian asks me. He is wearing a red bathrobe and leads me by the arm into a tiny office. Then he says, "I want you to wrestle for me."

"What?"

"I've got a mask." He pulls the mask out of his bathrobe pocket and throws it at me. I hold it. "No one will know it's you."

The mask is white with black coloring around the eyes.

"No."

He blinks. A large fan in the corner lifts the bangs high off of his forehead. "Think of Joseph Campbell."

"I'm pale and weak," I tell him.

"Exactly," he says, leaning closer. "Your vulnerability is a strength. The script has been rewritten for you. You're going to win tonight."

"No." I laugh.

"Just dance around with the guy for a few minutes and follow his lead. He knows what to do."

"Why don't you do it?"

"Because of my birthmark." He raises the robe and shows me the strange place, shaped like Africa, across his back. "I'm identifiable now," he says, "even with a mask."

He reaches into his pocket and pulls out one tiny, blue pill. "Even professional golfers take these now. All the stress will disappear."

"This whole thing," I swallow hard, holding the mask in one hand and the pill in the other. "Why in the world would I ever want to do this?"

"I don't know," he tells me, heading for the door. "But you do."

"Where are you going?"

"To finish rewriting the script," he says.

When I step from behind the curtain there is silence. Slowly I hear a mixed chorus of laughter and jeers. I can't see too well walking down the aisle— the mask is too big and tends to slide over my eyes. I feel my toes curl inside my red wrestling boots as I climb into the ring. Hiding in the corner,

I am wearing something very close to grippy underwear.

"LADIES AND GENTLEMEN," the loudspeaker announces, "PRUF-ROCK."

The curtain blows open and out gallops the largest man in mask I've ever seen. He is dressed in leather and slaps the crowd wildly as he enters. He steps over the top rope effortlessly.

The referee gestures for me to come to the center of the ring.

I stare at my opponent, who through the narrow slits of my mask suddenly looks eerily familiar. He must be seven feet tall. His skin sparkles in the lights, his hand like a starfish consuming mine.

"Your hands are so soft," he purrs.

Back and forth we dance, slinging each other against the scratchy ropes. In a headlock Prufrock hums sweetly in my ear. He slaps my face for real before drawing me closer again in a clinch. "Kick me hard in the balls, Sebastian," he whispers, "then wrap your legs around my throat and squeeze."

When he slings me again against the ropes I do exactly as I was told: I kick him in the balls and once he has fallen in the center of the ring I wrap my legs around his face.

Suddenly as if on cue the crowd rises, cheering for me now as though I were a racehorse, the only time in my whole life that I can remember being cheered at all. Adrenaline surges through my veins. I have never felt so strong. Between my legs Prufrock's eyes open widely underneath his mask. I am like Keats, I tell myself, my head spinning wildly. Lord Byron. The tighter I squeeze the louder the crowd cries. Prufrock makes a terrific show of trying to twist his body underneath mine, flailing his arms desperately, but my hold is too strong. When at last his eyes have closed and his arms have fallen sleepily to his sides, the referee raises his right arm and slaps the mat like a drum. The auditorium erupts. Not until then do I release my grip and realize slowly with a sickening feeling that Prufrock is not breathing at all.

Roper lives high up in the Avenues, a series of lettered, tree-lined streets surrounding the city's oldest cemetery. From his unmarked mailbox the Salt Lake skyline appears unexpectedly, draped with a moonlit miasma, a mirage in the snow. Looking down at the glowing valley, at the dark, silent

ring of the Wasatch mountain range, how long did it take, I wonder, before I took these mountains for granted? Three weeks? Five?

"Do you think Roper really used to manhandle Madonna?" Sebastian asks. His red raincoat flaps in the wind.

I ignore him.

"Maybe that silly, old song of hers is about him. I forget its name. Late at night I've heard it playing in his office, the poor bastard. Maybe *Rolling Stone* is right after all," he says. "Maybe Roper is the next Walt Whitman."

Every once in a while, after several beers, we find ourselves again in this quiet clearing, a pilgrimage that began two years earlier after a poetry reading, the first time we had ever pissed in David Roper's yard.

"It's not your fault," he tells me. "Prufrock is a lot older than he looks. His heart could give out at any time, poor bastard. Steroids." He spits. "At least that's what they're saying. I don't know him very well. Thank God the paramedics brought him back."

"In Japan more people die each year on stairwells than in fires," I say, bent over, nauseous, my head still buzzing.

"There is a poem in that somewhere."

"A strange man who looked a lot like Professor Roper almost died tonight between my legs," I say to him before standing up. "Is there something you're not telling me that I ought to know about?"

He opens Roper's mailbox and closes it.

"Alex Field is dead," Sebastian says.

"What?"

"He was found stabbed tonight in a classroom at Orson Spenser Hall. In a way it's a lucky thing," he tells me.

"When did this happen?"

"Just a few hours ago. I heard it over the radio."

"While I was wrestling?"

"Roughly, yes." He glances at me. "Surely you're not blaming yourself?"

"Sebastian," I say slowly, aware suddenly of how strange my voice sounds when upset and nervous.

He opens Roper's mailbox again and closes it.

"Did you know that there is a bird in this world that lays its eggs in the nests of other birds? It's a particularly aggressive kind of bird. Once hatched, in fact, it invariably kills the other hatchlings. The songbird is most vulnerable to this bird. Do you know why?" he asks in a different voice.

"No."

"Because of its song, of course. It brings them in." He opens and closes the mailbox again, his head remaining perfectly still. "I've thought about this an awful lot," he says carefully, turning to me, "and I think it must mean that we just don't like each other's work very much, that we don't feel threatened."

"What are you talking about?"

"Why we're friends." He opens his mouth and closes it, drawing the gun at his side, a different gun than the one before—smaller, less shiny. "Writers aren't supposed to be friends," he says just like that.

That's something Hemingway would have said to Fitzgerald, I think to myself, blowing on my hands, but I do not say it. I look up at the wet dropcloth of stars, so many that I begin to sway, my head spinning faster in the altitude.

"'Lucky Star,'" I hear myself say.

Sebastian stares at me, his brows lightly raised, the way he looks when reading a surprising poem.

"The song by Madonna," I tell him. "I've heard him humming it."

He turns his wolfish grin to the moon. "One more reason why I'd much prefer a black hole be named after me than a constellation any day." Like a leading man, he winks. "No matter the significance."

I turn to him and say very carefully, "You remembered my birthday."

"Bang."

As I recoil from the shot, I instantly feel myself being transformed, not unlike that of the thin wafer in Proust, by the release of a long-forgotten taste dripping coldly now down my chin—no, not blood. I spit, surprised. "Yoo-Hoo."

Sebastian takes off running. Hopping the fence and its new No Trespassing signs and following as fast as I can across Roper's backyard, I pretend I am the keeper and sole survivor of a small, quarantined city that shimmers at night. I run like I ran the bases as a child. The ground crackles beneath my feet. I think how small the Japanese are, their small bodies filling the stairwells, more and more of them, and how frightening it must be to be so small.

It's a cool, windy night, clouds racing across the moon's blank face, when I hear a familiar hum rising softly in the darkness, just as the tall figure steps out of the trees some twenty paces behind our backs and shines light down on us as though we were small boys pissing on the last patch of snow.

"It will happen like this," David Roper's hoarse voice cracks. "It is cast."

The sky falls gently in sharp, white pieces, making everything seem as if in slow motion. Sebastian buckles his pants. I notice his shoelaces are untied. Then he does something that shouldn't surprise me but it does: he pulls out the gun again from the inside of his coat.

"Don't," I whisper, ready to grab his wrist.

He raises his right arm and spins around. It's the second or the third pop, I think, that slams Sebastian's head back. His eyes swing around to look at me for an instant with extreme interest. Then his mouth falls open, just as the wind rattles the huddled trees.

Conceit

Summer a long time ago
When the lounge chair flipped
As you leaned back

With a drink in your hand.
The concentrated turning
And balancing of the body

While falling backwards
Onto the damp, tall grass,
Not spilling a drop.

"See," you said, rising
To your feet and holding
The glass forward. "Proof."

A month later at dawn, the morning of my thesis defense, a second envelope slides under my door. Tottering erect like a penguin from the mattress on the floor where Karen sleeps, I tear open the paper and out falls copies of four pictures: three of Karen in her bedroom posed in varying states of undress; and one of Derek Taylor, my former classmate, the first of us to die. It was taken very closely from the neck-up. He is trying to cover his face with one hand, but I can see that he is either laughing or crying, and I can also see the barest reflection in the round mirror behind him of

Karen leaning forward with the camera low at her waist, the sly, silver sheen of the light.

"Utah girls," reads the inscription penned with a smiley face on back of the envelope.

I watch Karen sleep from the rocking chair across the room. Her hair rests across her breasts like Audrey Hepburn's hands. After about every third breath her mouth opens and I think I hear her whisper, "Oh, my heck." Somewhere far away I can hear a truck backing up, the cackle of blackbirds on the balcony. Then, just like that, everything slows: Déjà vu. I close my eyes. "It's only your brain stopping and restarting," I remember my father telling me.

As if in a dream I tiptoe to the foot of the bed like a child. "Light flows from you," I whisper to her. "You are another nature."

As I reach to touch her big toe, Karen rears up and kicks me hard in the face. I reel backward over the coffee table. With long, horselike strides she pounces on me instantly, jamming three then four fingers down my throat, hissing. In her wake suddenly my arms are pinned under her knees, my neck nailed to the floor. Her strength is unnatural and breathtaking. I try to bite, but my night-guard is still in my mouth. She braces her knees and cocks her arms above me, her hair smelling of apricots as blood rushes to my brain— oxygen. I'm scared. The horrible hissing, I realize only now, is coming from inside of me. I'm scared. My fingertips tingle. Then my tongue begins to give. I feel myself turning slowly to the light and opening.

"Predictable, isn't it," a familiar voice interrupts, "that it is only in leaving that you grow sentimental for this quiet city in a valley, a little bit scared, perhaps, that the years you spent in Utah might have been two of your best?"

You close your eyes and see the young Lawrence in his white linen tunic. Only now do you notice that half his skull in back is missing. Tears chill your cheeks.

"Before this conversation inevitably turns," Sebastian whines, "as in a Jane Austen novel, to the weather and the condition of the road—"

Your legs feel strong on your bike. You glide down streets that you've never been on before, pedaling past large, dark houses cut deeply from the two-lane road, which gradually loosens to gravel, jolting your tires, as you move farther and farther away from the city, everything, even the wind, behind you.

"—How quiet you have become in death," you tell him. "It doesn't suit you at all."

"It's like being in a jazz group," he says, his deep voice farther and farther away, "playing in cheesy-tuxedo wedding gigs with a bunch of older guys who sit around all day cracking jokes about their wives…"

You zip through the fog. The cold air feels like water in your lungs.

"It will happen like this," sings the bird. "This is the beginning."

Just when you think you can ride forever, you stop.

Off the road to the right, against a sharp cliff of stone, is an opening you've seen before. "It's a secret tunnel." Water drains out of it into a trench, and when you climb inside you bump your head against the concrete top, your voice echoing down a long, dark corridor, the end of which is lit straight in front of you, not less than a hundred feet away. You step over the trickle and walk to the end, where, it is true, you see giraffes loping across an open field, the sky looming with low, thin clouds when dust on the horizon turns into birds again.

MATE

by AARON GWYN

DENNIS AND I are playing chess when the guards bring Jingo in. His name is Jingo because this is what someone yells from the first tier. *Hey,* the voice yells, *look at this Jingo.* Our tier is the second, and there is a third and fourth above. We stare out onto an expanse of concrete and across the expanse, a control room where the guards stare back. There is the control room, and there are railed walkways (our side and theirs), and the men pace back and forth behind their rails, back and forth in front of ours, back and forth and back and forth in their tan and brown uniforms with PCI stenciled on their patches and PCI on their badges of shiny brass and AR-15s braced against the shined buckles above their hips. Those rifles are saying, *go ahead and see, why don't you. Go ahead and see.*

Jingo is short, and Jingo is white, and Jingo is headed for Tier One, Cell Fifteen, and this cell is where they keep the new fish for psychiatric observation, and they don't do a psych screen unless you aren't cut out for PCI, and Jingo is definitely not. I don't know what he could be cut out for. I don't know if it exists. We watch him, small and pale, the color of boiled egg. We keep watching until he disappears under the landing and is locked into the cell beneath us. Inmates are howling his newly given name. They

are yelling *come on,* and they are yelling *come here,* and one yells that Jingo has a party coming, and I ask Dennis *is this true?*

Dennis just shakes his massive head.

He puts a finger atop his bishop and his eyes cross from staring.

"I ain't taking on any more," he tells me. "I got my hands full with you."

I've been here six weeks. I don't belong. Dennis saw it right away, and he swept above me a tattooed limb. He has Grim Reaper and he has 88. He has Swastika, and White Power, and OKC Hammers. Thorns and bullets. Bits of barbed wire. He talks constantly. Six weeks and I've heard his life sixty-one times. He snores when he's asleep and the bunk rattles. He's on crystal meth and pills. A guard named Miller brings him a package every day and every day he offers and I every day I say no. He's six feet five inches, two hundred eighty-five pounds. He can bench-press his body weight thirteen times. I've counted the reps.

Me, I'm five-ten, one eighty-nine. I'm getting bigger. I weigh myself every day. I've lost fifteen pounds of fat. I've put on at least that much muscle. I can see it in my arms and chest. Rec time and I'm out with the Skins at the weight pile and we spot each other and trade quips. I'm keeping myself tight and gathered. I'm keeping myself tucked away. When they asked what kind of name was Peters, I didn't say Jewish. I didn't tell them about challah bread or my marketing degree from Northwestern. I didn't tell them last year I made close to two hundred thousand and lived on the south side of Tulsa. That I had a pool and a porch swing. A lab named Mitzvah. When they asked what kind of name was Peters, I told them American.

Dennis says that that's good.

He says that's the best kind.

It's twenty-hour lockdown here at Perser Correctional, but you can only sleep maybe ten. Sometimes you can't sleep at all. Sometimes you lie on your tray and your mattress is a half-inch pallet of vinyl and you listen to Dennis and it all runs together. My therapist would have said ADD, but I don't think that's going to help. Dennis talks and I listen and if I can get to the part where it's just fluorescent-light humming, then I can make it to my next appeal. It won't be forever.

I told Dennis my third day inside. We were sitting on his bunk mixing Kool-Aid and soaking toilet paper.

"Dennis," I told him. "Dennis, I don't belong."

He just kept soaking and mixing, toothbrush down in the purple dye. He said that neither did he.

I shook my head. Told about the trial and charges. Told about Mark Richards.

"What *is* manslaughter?" I asked him. "What does that mean?"

"Means," said Dennis, "that you slaughtered a man."

He stood from his cot and set the mix aside. He knelt down and started a set of push-ups. I sat and watched him, keeping the count.

At sixty-five he began grunting. At eighty a vein between his eyebrows went blue and forked down from his hairline. In the health club back in Tulsa, I exercised alone. I'd look around the room and see the expressions on everybody. The big hair and bad skin. People stepping over each other. People in a quarrel over the last plates. All these people flexing and popping gum, the whole tanning-bed lot of them like a burnt orange clench in my stomach. Sometimes I'd vomit and sometimes I'd cry. Sometimes I'd go sit in traffic and it'd be all cell phones and blinkers, speed bumps and horns. I'd try to picture a place other than everywhere I'd ever been, people other than all I'd ever known. I thought if I could find the right people, it wouldn't be as wrong.

Dennis pushed his way to one-twenty-five. He stopped, stood, then sat back on the cot. He was dry and white, his head so shaved I could see myself mirrored. Like a funhouse reflection. Like something gone smeared.

We made our chess mat out of cardboard box. We made the pieces from toilet paper. We'd dab the paper under the faucet of the toilet-sink unit and then press the pieces into knights and kings and bishops and rooks. Dennis's pawns all look the same, and with the paper dry, they even have a marbled finish. For the knights he works the horse's face with the sharpened tip of the toothbrush. They have fierce eyes and long nostrils and for manes a mohawk of fifteen spikes. Mine don't look as good, but Dennis shows me where to press and pinch. When they're dry, we mix Kool-Aid, grape and cherry, and we color one set of pieces purple and the other set of pieces red. Dennis says red will be white and purple, black.

"White moves first," he says.

When I ask why not just leave one set uncolored he stares at me.

"White always move first," he says.

Dennis wins every game. He says I have a tendency to hide away my king.

I worry about being here, about sticking it out. Only college graduate in the facility and that includes Warden Stiles. There's an unfriendly room waiting for me and I think constantly beyond the fence. I want to be around others like myself, maybe twenty or ten. Lonely here and loud and no one ever says please. I'm sleepy all the time, which beats, I suppose, sick and angry, which was all I ever used to be. In the cubicle. Then the office. One day I stapled the inside of my arm. I did six more like a railroad or monster. I was first pick out of two hundred applicants and after three months I was suturing my bicep where there weren't any cuts.

It's like Rabbi Hemmers used to say about marriage: find your fit and you slide into place.

Find someone else's and you're good as stuck.

Jingo's second day a special doctor comes to see him twice. A guard brings him his meals and another brings him books and magazines. Dennis says this treatment is going to get Jingo a party. It's already here.

Third Tier is Mister Roy's. The party's coming from him. Roy looks to the brothers and if you aren't a brother, and someone isn't looking to you, you belong to Mister Roy plain and pat. No negotiations. No special cases or pleas. Isn't racism or politics or fashion. Simple economics. Sort and sift. Skins have the weight pile, Latinos the yard. Brothers take the courts, and this is theirs just like a pink slip or mortgage. You could say things should be some other way, but they are this way instead.

Jingo's third day the doctor is back, and on the fourth we watch him come again. He comes for two weeks, and then word is the psych screen is over. Jingo will be moved to a regular cell. Regular cell with regular mate. There is talk about where he will be housed, but talk is all. We know where Jingo is going. He's been going since the moment he walked in.

Jingo is manacled in handcuffs and chains, led up the steel steps from Tier One to Three. We can see him climbing, his face blanched, eyes the size of saucers. He is taken up, unlocked, placed inside with Mr. Roy. It was quiet while he walked, stockroom still, but now the door slides to a

volley of yammers and bleats. It comes from everywhere at once, all around, inmates shouting, wanting life, wanting death, wanting *rape and torture; torture, rape.*

I am frightened by the timbre and volume, the shouters white and black. By Dennis shouting and laughing and stamping his feet. Hands on the bars, cheeks wedged in the gap, he stomps and shouts and I am frightened. Eyes gone red, skin gone red, the floor underneath me tremble, tremble. These are the moments I can't get away. I cannot move, then I cannot stop. Everything is fear and angles: concrete, glass, elbows, gravel, and teeth. Dennis gets bigger and bigger, louder and bigger, large as lung cancer. I am frightened he is shouting, and frightened what he shouts. I am frightened right beside him, shouting louder than the rest.

Lights out, we lie in the gray and whisper to each other like a couple in bunk beds, like a sleepover or camp. It is midnight now and the party's about to start.

"You awake?" I ask Dennis.

"Yeah," he says. "You?"

A moment passes.

"I need to learn to castle."

"You need to what to what?"

"Castle," I tell him. "I never swap the king."

"Swap it," he says.

"Is it one space or two?"

"Either way."

"Either direction?"

"You can move him one space or two."

We lie there. Dennis taps his toe against a rung at the bottom, soft, muffled clanks.

Out beyond the bars, it is quiet. Everyone waiting and whispering. There won't be any shouting this time.

I turn to one side. Then I turn on the other. I am finally about to doze when I first think I hear. I slide up on my elbows and stare at the ceiling. It's eight inches away and I can feel my breath bouncing back.

"You hear that?" I ask.

"No."

"You hear it now?"

"Yes."

We stop and listen. Dennis stops tapping his toe.

"You can't castle out of check," he tells me.

"I what?"

"If you're in check you can't castle. You don't get to move that way."

I nod even though I know he can't see. I nod again and try and think of anything to say back, try and keep it going, but the party is louder now, and my mind just goes flat.

I count fifteen minutes before Dennis whispers, "Stan?"

"What?" I ask him.

"You awake?"

"Yeah."

"Don't pay attention to that."

"Yeah?"

"Don't pay attention."

"Yeah," I say, and then the party's suddenly over, and the weeping turns to sobs. My throat gets small and tight.

"How long is he going to keep that up?" I ask him.

"Keep what up?"

"How long?"

"Don't worry about it."

"Don't worry?"

"You know the song."

"Which?"

"It's his party," sings Dennis.

"Yeah," I tell him, but neither of us laughs.

The next morning when we're called onto our porches for count, the guards do a cell search and take away our chess. Miller comes by later to drop a package and apologize, says one of his colleagues took the pieces home to his niece. When the lieutenant leaves, we have to start them all over.

We start, this time, with the kings. Dennis thinks we ought to make them like us, red him, purple me, our expressions, our build. He takes the tip of his toothbrush and begins to poke and press. He scrapes the pectorals, then the arms crossed just beneath, the legs below, the knees and feet. Two more hours and the king is naked but for a helmet: nude Teutonic warrior with a crown of massive horns. He cuts the features, the eyebrows and nose, the mouth a sharpened scream. He stretches his shoulders and sets the piece to dry. Looks over at me and grins.

"Mine," he says, and he's right. It's his exactly and over the next week he makes an entire court. Naked pawns, naked horsemen, naked bishops and rooks. The queen is also naked, but she wears a headdress of tiny snakes. Look at the pieces and you know right away. This is *his* assembly. He is *their* king. Red-white is an impressive set.

Purple, however. Purple is different.

Chain mail and armor. Lots of that. Great plates of iron, well hammered and thick. The bodies behind could be any size—midgets pulling levers and gears—but the surfaces are wide and substantial. The gloved hands carry halberds, great broadswords slung on the backs. The helmets have cheek guards, chin guards, a visor for each. All you can see is the straight line of their mouths. When I get to the king, I try and outfit him the same, but he keeps coming out smaller than the others, wrong. I can't get his feet and I can't get his face and there's a problem, I think, with the look of his hands. What I come up with is unshapely and blank. His troopers are fine, his woman is fine, but he himself could as easily be stable keep, a boy servant or slave. He could be some kind of profession that doesn't exist.

I blow-dry the paper and place it between the bars to catch air from the breezeway. I turn him about-face.

Dennis studies him a moment.

"Looks just like you," he says.

Three days later, and the party goes on. We haven't slept much and we don't really eat. Dennis gulps the pills harder and even I down a few, and one evening, just after mess, the lights take a hydrocodone shimmer, and we begin to talk. We talk about work, and we talk about life, how we got here and where we got going. Dennis snorts the powder; I listen and advise; and in the wee hours, party full blare, we demonstrate everything that we know.

He describes a detonator, and I'm with my hands in front of me, finger-ing a clarinet. He shows proper push-ups, how to shine shoes with a banana peel, how to roll dental floss in Comet and saw into steel. I talk him

through all the lessons I ever took: tennis, jujitsu, ice-skating, and tap. I talk five years karate, three years Latin; kickboxing, piano, kali, first aid. How I competed, one winter, as a cross-country skier, tore a hamstring, fractured a rib. Dennis has more interest in certain things. He wants to know how to submit someone with the lapel of his gi.

I show him the six positions of Brazilian jujitsu, a string of various chokes. I show him triangle and rear-naked, how to defend the guillotine, how to reverse an arm bar. He takes it all in and we swallow and sniff. The weeping upstairs is some other muzak, some other different life. Dennis and I spar and grapple. We wrestle and spin.

Later, lying in our racks, we pass the pills and I tell him about the trial. Mark Richards, the outdoor retreat. How he came towards me, swinging to kill. How in two minutes he was gone.

My attorney argued self-defense. At a conference in Houston, colleagues had seen Mark threaten my life. They took the stand and said, "at the conference in Houston, we saw him threaten Stan's life."

The judge and jury, they saw it different. They saw two prior arrests and two stints in rehab. They saw Xanax and Paxil and a pocket of painkillers that hadn't been prescribed. They didn't see snow skiing. They didn't see piano and tap. They saw black belts and state medals. They saw drunk and disorderly, simple assault, the length of the knife I carried with my laptop. They saw the video of a grappling tournament where I gouged a man's eyes.

My lawyer, I tell Dennis, came to me. He came to me and said I had a ninety-percent chance of walking away. The other ten was first-degree murder and lethal injection. I could risk it or sign a plea. Sign, and you do eighteen months. Risk, and they hook you up to the dying machine.

I decided sign, but I decide now I should have decided different. If now were then and I knew what I know.

"What?" Dennis interrupts from below me. "What do you know?"

"What do I know?"

"What do you know?"

I think about this for several minutes.

"What it's like," I tell him. "I know what it's like."

"What's it like?"

"What's what like?"

"What you're talking about."

"I'm just talking."

"So am I."

I tell him I don't understand.

"You said," says Dennis, "if you knew what it was like you would've risked it."

"Right."

"Something so bad it's bad enough to risk."

"Okay."

"Death's better."

"Right."

"You'd rather die."

"That's right."

"So?" he asks.

"So what?"

"So, what's it like?"

"The *it* I'd rather not be in?"

"Yeah."

"The *it* I'd rather die?"

"Yes."

"This," I say, my voice suddenly rising, "it's exactly like goddamned this."

There are a few quiet moments, and I can feel an inch of heat around me like the aching from a burn, a terry cloth towel scalding my face. I lean my eyes over the bunk and stare into dark. Even though Dennis has looked to me, he's still just a thief. Just a skinhead and a bigot and a junkie and a hood. He has no diplomas. He has no front teeth. He's a drug addict and a felon and he was raised in projects by his uncle and aunt. As an infant, he had beer in his bottle. They put cigarettes out on the balls of his feet.

Filthy, I'm thinking. Filthy and out of sorts. Not one thing in his life any better than the others. Not one thing good enough to make a stand. How does it get to this? How did he let it? I've been trying to make it, but sometimes you get tired of pretend. You get tired and isn't it obvious? Skinhead and burglar and these papers of meth? Twenty hours a day in a six-by-eight cell. Don't have to go any further. Right there and you're better off dead.

Below me the room is still quiet. It'll be that way until he stands. He'll slide to his feet and grab me by the crotch. He'll put my skull to the concrete and a boot to my throat. He outweighs me, out-lifts me, so it'll take everything I've got. I'll have to bridge up on the small of my back. I'll have to slip the tip of the toothbrush repeatedly into his ear.

I am waiting, ready, thighs tensed, fingers gripping plastic. I am ready to drop a bunk and think preemptive when Dennis begins to snore.

Bright morning, sunlight and ceiling tile. Out in the corridor, they're calling us for count.

We step onto the grilled platform of Tier Two, I to the right side, Dennis to the left. The guards will call and we'll answer back. Last name. D.O.C. number. If you forget or stumble, they give you a citation. Three citations, they take away your privileges. My first week, I practiced the number like a recipe or prayer.

Dennis's eyes are straight ahead. My eyes are straight. I am thinking about the night before, thinking what he will remember, trying to remember myself, piece it back together, my stomach washed and my eyes heavy from the pills. I think this and I think my number, and then I stop thinking, and there is commotion above. A guard is yelling for Jingo, but Jingo does not answer back. I look up through the grilled walkway and see the soles of Mr. Roy's boots. Then a sash of white flits across, a rumbling at the rails. There is pounding on concrete, pounding on the walkway, and then someone shouts, and then I see him. It is Jingo above me, suspended in air. Eyes blank, face blank, a length of sheet knotted around his throat. The other end has been knotted at the rail and he has launched himself from Tier Three, run, planted a foot, and leapt. He is vaulted, arms tucked, white form against concrete and shadow. He looks like the statue of something. He looks like stone. All that motion and all that expanse. I am rooting he will continue, that this will be his life now, that now he will be this. A constellation in our heaven. This lone figure in sky.

The thought is encouraging, but it cannot last. Gravity will betray him and already it tugs him to earth. He falls, thirty-two feet per second, the thirty-seven inmates on Tier Two all leaning out to watch. His body straightens, toes pointed, hands at his sides as if jumping in a pool. I wonder how long is the sheet, and then it is two sheets, three. I am counting for a fourth knot when the sheet tightens and goes entirely stiff. Jingo's body

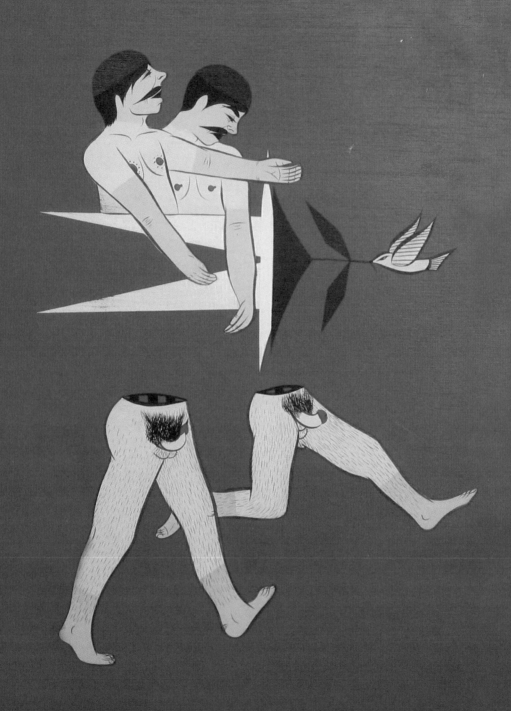

gives a shudder, his shins swing to clank against our railing, and there he droops, ear to his shoulder. He doesn't look peaceful. He doesn't look scared. What he looks like is gone. Thirty-six inmates on Tier Two all stare at their feet. No one shouts or howls. No one coughs. They all just want him away.

Me, I'm not done. There are things I'm here to determine and this isn't my first corpse. The other I only saw from the back. There was the back of his head as I pushed it away, his face planted in the green tufted grass. Jingo, however; Jingo turns. He pivots back and forth on the end of his sheet. For the first time I realize he is naked, his body white and pink, his face a dark magenta, the blood collected there. His bowels have gone, plus his bladder, and his mouth is all ajar. He looks like the symbol of something, but I cannot figure what. Jingo dead and at the end of his sheet should be a symbol, there should be meaning, and I run through all the things he could be a symbol of, an entire catalogue. He hangs there and turns, and it is not a pleasant sight. I stare at him and cannot look away. He is going to give me something. I will not let him go. He hangs and turns, hangs and turns, and I go through my catalogue and try to force a fit. I try and push, try and strain, my whole spine tensed toward it, my toenails and my fingers curled. Then there is collapsing, a grating and a click. Something gives way. Right above my palate. In that space behind your eye. I look at Jingo once more before turning. There are people who say they'd rather be dead, but truth is they wouldn't. Truth is, they'd rather be anything else.

I glance over at Dennis and he shakes his massive head.

"Poor fucker," he tells me. "I wish we could've brought him aboard."

We sit, Dennis and I, on the bottom bunk. He offers drugs and I take all he gives. They've sanctioned a twenty-four-hour lockdown, and it'll be that way for the next several months. Events like Jingo's have a way of multiplying. The warden foresees a rail of inmates, all of us dangling from the ends of our sheets. One, he can bowl over and bury. Thirty, and they move us to Big Mac. It hits the papers and the talk shows and the taxpayers' pockets. Stiles has to ponder his vocation, if he's found the right fit.

Over the week, Miller brings pills and packages, decks of cards and novels and dice. Dennis wants to know will I read to him. Wants to know will I show him how. The answer is sure, but I want, first thing, to get back to the chess. I want him to teach me all that he knows.

I want to learn to align the bishops, stagger the pawns, the right time to release the queen, how to position her with knights. I want to know the rooks, their assist to a blockaded bishop, their application in forcing a draw. I want to know Fool's Mate and its proper defense—Dennis has caught me forty-one times.

Mainly, I want to know the king, how to move him with his court. I don't want him castled. I don't want him crowded by rooks. He may slide only one space, but he takes any bearing, and he can capture just like a pawn. The queen's our bad girl, *domina nocturna,* and Dennis makes her sparkle and spank. The king, though. Lose him and play is ended. Lose him and banish the board.

I'm working him slowly with a toothpick I bartered. Cost me two packs of cigarettes and three cans of cocktail, but every evening I hunch on my bunk and listen to Dennis, and he's talking Aryan Brotherhood, or he's talking squats, or he's telling me about that time in Laredo, how he almost started the Riot. I sit and I listen and it's like Father in his rocking chair, the radio tuned to NPR. I wet the end of the toothpick and carve angles, make lines, work the body, work the face, try, for once, to get it right. I look at his court lined on a shelf across the room, and I try to imagine what their king would look like. Who their king would be.

I used to look at the cube of cardboard we'd made into our quadrant, the lines drawn and the squares colored with ballpoint ink. The lines were never even. There was a barcode stamped along one corner, the board dented, the surface marked with grease. I used to think about my pieces against those scribbled squares. I used to pick them up and set them down lightly, not wanting to slide them, not wanting anything to rub off. Now, when the king moves, he digs in at his base. He digs in and walks over, feet planted, the purple boots, light armor, light purple robes. The robes have black smears where he's stumbled past horses, tripped over foot soldiers, leaned against the stones of a besieged castle's walls. He wears no helmet and only a diadem for a crown. His hair is shoulder length, and even now, the court arrays before him, and across the field an army is stained red in the day's final light. There is a battle brewing, the stamp and nicker of horses, a breeze among the patches of grass. A horn blows, and the first line charges, the king behind them, pressed at their backs. He has outstripped the queen and nobles. His cavalry and castles have yet to catch up. He runs towards his rival, eyes focused forward, his garments soiled with the soil of his world, robes brushing slough edge and shadow, trailing behind him a purple smear.

THE KING'S BOOK

by SAM MILLER

DEAR AMYTIS,

Today I had a visit in my cell from some very self-important men who had many questions which, presumably, they thought to be very provocative and profound, but which ultimately bored me and took me away from the work that has become all I have left: my most recent novel. Dedicated, of course, to you.

In a way, this has been a fortunate incarceration. I am relieved of the burden of fugitive living: the paranoia and the dirt smells, the feeling of having retired into an earth grave, the half-death of it. My cell here, at least, is clean. It is simple and bare, a décor to which I am unaccustomed, but which has proven to be inspirational. Apart from the distractions of glamour and adulation and responsibility, during these long hours of desolate silence, I have single-mindedly meditated on you, and the rich fantasy life that used to inform my fiction has begun to revisit me. I look around: dusty floor, springy bed, poster of my friends and colleagues, high ceiling, lone dome light. The glossy white tiles on the walls reflect the spot of light from the ceiling so that they seem to be translucent. The walls themselves have become like windows through which I glimpse the other land where this novel takes place.

I envision you as a peasant girl married to a boorish man in ancient Tikrit. I am a powerful king. I pass you at the well in disguise and say, simply, *"Marhaba,"* and you look into my eyes, seeing me for who I am, and reply, *"Al hamdu lillah."* With my simple cypress staff I sketch a symbol in the sand on the ground. You see it only briefly before it is whisked away by the desert wind to commingle with grains from other lands; to blow across plains with other sands. The hidden meaning of this symbol, this character that I trace in the dust, is that you and I will meet later in the night under the crystalline stars in the palms outside the village. There under heaven we will fornicate wildly, and you will forget your husband and your maudlin wifely duties. You understand the meaning behind the symbol and you pledge with silent eyes through your burka to be there no matter the risk.

Today I recorded this scene on a piece of the parchment I demanded from my captors. It culminates in the following passage regarding our union:

> "Oh yes!" she cried, "YES!" as he thrust his throbbing member into her velvety sheath. She writhed in pleasure on the pillows as he entered her again and again, thanking Allah that she had the privilege of making love to the most powerful man on Earth.

I have requested a copy of *The Old Man and the Sea.* I want to get back to the books that made me want to write in the first place. The spare beauty of Hemingway's prose is akin to the beauty of the desert, and I have been pining to see the desert.

At any rate, it was during the birth of this chapter that the men arrived at my cell. I recognized one of them, Mowaffak al-Rubaie. He was one of many turncoats upon whom I was inclined to mete out justice during my glorious reign. The American General and Ambassador were there, escorted by American Rangers. I asked them to come back at another time as I was in the middle of something. Truthfully, I wanted to pleasure myself. I was lost in the fantasy of you, Amytis. I was transported to that ancient land, I was *there,* and I was perturbed to have been jerked out of it, so to speak.

Al-Rubaie walked right up to my table, to my stack of paper, and rifled through it. I suppose he enjoyed taking this privilege with me. It would have earned him his death a few years ago. Seeing his pudgy fingers smudge the manuscript, I wanted to kill him. I wanted to torture him all over again.

He lifted a page and asked what it was. "Fiction? Is it really?" he said, "Romance? You are writing a romance book?" The leaf of paper shook in his hand, I noticed. He was trying to hide behind a quiet diplomat's voice and posture. I have never had the patience for that kind of posing. But he had more to say! "After the crimes you have committed against humanity? After the people you killed? This is what comes to you?"

As a man, he disgusts me. He has so little understanding about that of which he speaks, but he has so much vitriol. He is ignorant and little and beneath me.

"Did you ask their relatives what they had done, these people?" I asked him. "They were thieves, or they escaped from the battlefield." Amytis, you know this to be the truth. You know that I was just. I never served anyone with an unjust sentence. I am a reasonable and purposeful king.

He dropped the page he was reading and it seesawed down through the air like a dying bird. I wonder: would he have tossed aside a page of the Quran so dismissively?

"You must be having a perfectly joyous time with this, al-Rubaie, you pile of shit," I said. He perked up hearing me speak his name. Amytis, he should consider it a blessing that the base word passed my lips.

"You remember me then? Do you remember the order when you gave it?" He still couldn't look me in the face. Even though I am defeated in fact, I am powerful, victorious in mind and spirit.

"Do I remember? I remember you as a task I accomplished once on a busy day. Don't flatter yourself. You are a street bitch to me. I remember you like a fucking dog I once ran over on the way to work. Did the torture leave scars? Did the confinement make you sad and lonely? What do I care? What have you done for me lately?" I remembered this last line from an American pop song. I have always liked the ring of it. One of the qualities of my writing that has earned me critical praise is the sound of my words, the snap of my phrasing, like a good jazz singer.

Al-Rubaie hemmed and hawed and an American soldier stepped forward, but the other men hung back behind him, giving him his chance. I sensed that I would be victorious in this encounter.

"Al-Rubaie, take what revenge you can on me now, while I am underfed

and alone and unarmed. If that will make you feel like a big boy, go ahead and do it. The people gave me the power I had, and they will give it back. They like me, al-Rubaie, and you can't take that from me. Now is your time to do what you wish, away from their eyes."

I glared at him, feeling the burn in my stare. I felt the old power rising in my belly. Amytis, I was suddenly mad with passion for you. I felt young and strong again. I felt a rush through the meat of my muscles. I felt myself grow larger, and saw these poor specimens of Arab shrink before me.

And then a strange thing happened. Although my eyes were open, it was as if I was seeing our story again, but it was beyond my control. It was inventing itself. I had a vision in which I destroyed these men with my powerful arms. I split them to pieces. Then I tore open the fabric of time with blood-slick hands, stepped through a ragged portal into a strange temporal oviduct, and returned to Babylon as your historical Nebuchadnezzar. I saw myself throw you down upon the harem pillows in our palace and penetrate you with an enormous phallus. Inside this giant organ the holy homunculi of my descendants swam: Evilmerodach, Belshazzar, Cyrus, the whole legendary lineage. I peered at these micro-scopic men from a great height, examining them, sorting them out, and finally I saw myself, the most potent and promising of the million sperm. I sent that one on its way into the future, back through the temporal oviduct and into the desert, into the unworthy womb of my mother. I saw her in our village near Tikrit beating her abdomen and cutting herself with a kitchen knife, crying, "In my belly I'm carrying a satan!" as she is storied to have done. But she was not powerful enough to prevent me, and the love of the people stayed her hand and jacketed me from her abuse.

As I reached the point of the consummation of our lovemaking, as I was overtaken by ecstasy and the homunculi spewed endlessly forth from my member into your galactic womb of worlds, I saw myself burst out of my mother in an explosion of gore, fully grown and terrible. I shook off the birth-stuff like a dog shaking off water, I wiped the slime out of my mustache with a thumb, and I rose to a golden throne surrounded by angels. Next to the throne was a golden end table, on top of which sat a golden telephone. The golden telephone rang loudly and I set down a golden scepter to answer it. When I spoke hello, I heard the voice of Mowaffak al-Rubaie.

This is how I awoke from my prophetic daydream. "There are hundreds of thousands of people out in the streets now, rejoicing and celebrating your capture," al-Rubaie was saying. His voice was distant and irrelevant and incongruous. "Shall we take you and hand you over to these people? They will eat you alive."

"They are thugs, hooligans, gangsters," I said. Now he dared to look me in the eye. I was not angered. One doesn't punish a retarded child for speaking out of turn: it doesn't know better; hasn't the capacity to learn.

Al-Rubaie gestured at the American General and Ambassador. I was really working him up. His voice quivered and his pitch rose. "When they captured you, you did not shoot a single bullet against them," he said, "You had two Kalashnikov AK-47 machine guns and a pistol on your hip yet you did not fire, you held out your hands and surrendered, and offered to negotiate. You claim to be an Arab brave man. You are a coward."

Amytis, we both know this to be a false accusation, but I cannot stand to be called a coward. No one since my uncle forty years ago has spoken to me this way and come away unscathed. I turned my cheek away from him and looked back to my book. The words danced on the page illegibly, somehow come to life. I have not known that sort of confusion before.

"May God curse you in this life and in the hereafter," al-Rubaie said.

I focused on the words on the page and they rearranged themselves into sensible phrases. I spotted some corrections I would need to make. Somehow my time in the spider hole gave me better insight into what makes good literature. Amytis, I have decided that this will be my greatest novel ever. It will cause the entire Muslim world to rise up in a passion and destroy the invaders in a frenzied climax, an orgy of holy vengeance. We will cleanse the world of these pale vampires who seek to reduce us to husks, and in the end you will be with me, surrounded by our people: loved, loving, rejoicing, and my words will lull us as an empire into the bliss of postcoital slumber.

Al-Rubaie and the rest had a Ranger open the door and they walked out one at a time. Al-Rubaie was the last to go, and he stood there, apparently unsatisfied. I shouted a few f-words and b-words at him. He worked his jaw mawkishly like a sick, stupid fish, chewing on unanswered questions, glancing out the door at his cohorts as if to ask for more time. I made a face at him and turned back to my writing, back to you.

This thing will thread itself in with the rest of the threads of this time, Amytis. These laughable men will never have even a ghost of a notion of how history will record my legacy. This is an era governed by clock seconds and calendar years, and as for me and my line, we are bound by no such restraints. These ridiculous scuttling men will scuttle like bugs into their graves. They will decompose and crumble and my earth will purge itself of them, trailing their flaming dust through space like a comet.

CELEBRANTS

by CORINNA VALLIANATOS

We cornered Margo in the living room. She'd just left Sam. "Why now?" Dahlia asked. Her glasses, perfectly round, and her expression—as if she were searching, perpetually, for something wily and distant—lent her the appearance of a person peering through binoculars. "Why ever? You and Sam seem destined for great things."

Margo smiled and said, "Seemed."

"This is serious," I said. "Your life is serious."

She ignored me, turning to Dahlia with the smoothness, the sullenness, of a mannequin rotating in a shop window. "To answer your question—I've come to hate certain of his gestures, elemental things. The way he swallows, for instance. The way he aspirates."

"You're breaking up with Sam because you don't like the way he swallows and breathes?" I asked. It sounded perfectly reasonable, actually—it was the timing that I objected to.

Sam belonged to a club called the Reenactors, about which I felt a great deal of scorn and curiosity. The club had many ceremonies, the better to intrigue people like me. One of these ceremonies, due to take place in a week, was an official welcoming of members' girlfriends into the inner sanctums. Margo had already received her invitation.

"Oh dear," Dahlia said, as Margo walked away. We could hear her footfalls on the stairs. "She was going to memorize every detail of the ceremony according to mnemonic devices. Who was there, the timbre of the music, the oaths of fealty. I get dizzy just thinking of it going on without her."

I began to pace around. There was something dense and appealing about Dahlia, like a good wet piece of clay. "I can bear my own disappointment, but I can't bear yours," she said.

"I'm not disappointed," I said. "Do you know why?"

"Why?" Dahlia asked obediently.

"Sam's always liked you. He's always noticed you. I don't think you'd have to work very hard to win him over, especially when he's in such a vulnerable state."

She came toward me sawing a finger in front of her lips. "Margo can hear everything we're saying!"

"She sleeps with a pillow over her head."

"You're assuming she's asleep. You're assuming I'd want to woo Sam and be inducted into his silly club!"

"Not inducted. *Welcomed.*" I've noticed that arguments can be won by substituting details where substance should be. "Think about it. I'd do it, but Margo's told me he's freaked out by me."

"What about you?" Dahlia asked.

"My general demeanor, for some reason. Listen. Will you try?"

"If it'll make you happy…"

I thought about it. Not happy so much as satisfied, a less exalted feeling but infinitely more familiar.

The Reenactors occupied a lovely brick building with white columns and foul bathrooms in which eighteen-to-twenty-one-year-olds imbibed mixed drinks with a bravado that bordered on hysteria. I sipped beer out of a plastic cup, Dahlia by my side. Sometimes a fire burned in the fireplace and the little marble busts on the mantle were made to wear comedy and tragedy masks; other times the hearth was cold and dead and the action of the party outside, above, on the roof and overloaded balconies. It was then that I'd sit down, and listen to the distant raucous voices and try to discern which was Margo's, which Dahlia's (for she would have left me, been swept away by an admirer), and not be able to, and feel lonesomeness as a display of character, as if I were suffering onstage.

Club members had once staged events of decisive, even poetic, history: the first pebble cast by an Athenian in a democratic vote, Oppenheimer's disavowal of the nuclear bomb. But the charter had been amended, club dues reduced, the makeshift stage where reenactments had taken place fallen to a colony of termites. Now members were required only to reenact their own college years. Of course, they were still living out those years—but this was seen as a lucky coincidence, lending their performances authenticity and casting everything they said in a certain smart and dire light. They threw parties; they rehashed the particulars of the parties (carpets singed, a bathtub pitched from a third-floor balcony) in the lazy late hours of the next morning. Rumor had it that members of The Reenactors recorded, in a black felt book with a quill pen, for future casting purposes, the approximate height and weight and outstanding physical characteristic of every single person who passed through the club's front doors. If that was true, I felt sure there was a question mark next to my notations. Why did I go to those parties, why pretend? I suppose it was for Dahlia (Margo drifted around in a cloud of members, supported and hemmed in). It was so she'd have somewhere to go. I didn't need it but she did. She was too loyal to realize that, without me, she'd have had a much better time.

We had theories, certain suspicions. That a red hat worn on a member with brown hair meant something totally different than a blue hat worn on a member with blond hair. That the haiku on the bathroom stalls contained directions to a cache of cocaine, and that the beautiful Scandinavian woman who circulated at every social event was actually a male philosophy professor. These were the things Margo had been poised to find out.

The last party we'd attended at the club was called Our Living Systems. It was an homage to biology class. The air smelled of formaldehyde, and on a low table there was a display of a ram's horn, some coral, and a wasp's nest like a massive, ruined wad of gum. A few mice had been released, the idea being that wherever there was biology class there were mice, little disease bags. Dahlia and I were trying to capture them in order to take them outside and make them properly free. I didn't approve of this in-house wildness, not one bit.

Suddenly, Dahlia lurched toward a corner and held up a mouse by its

tail. It seemed to swim in the air, and as the small paws paddled it gained a horizontal position. It sniffed ardently. I felt an explosion of sympathy.

"I'll take that." A boy called the Grouper for his recessed chin and protuberant lower lip snatched the mouse away from Dahlia. He lowered it into a cup and turned the cup upside down on his head, and as the mouse struggled against his scalp a few drops of blood seeped out from under the rim and stood, lush as ink, on the ends of his hair. He smiled, beatific. Sam and Margo approached us.

"War paint!" Sam said.

The Grouper nodded soddenly.

Margo pinched my elbow. "You feel uncomfortable here, and so you take the rodent's side. Your heart just pours out to your fellow-oppressed."

She was exactly right. "Nonsense," I said.

"We were simply trying to release the mice into the wild," Dahlia said.

"I know *you* were," Margo answered.

The Grouper was the least attractive member of The Reenactors and for that reason—unspoken, immutable—he was the physical jokester, the prank-player. Wiping blood from his brow, he took the cup off his head and pretended to swallow its contents. Sam frowned in disapproval, nodding toward me.

"I'm not the keeper of the animals," I said. "Do whatever you like."

"You're the keeper's *conscience*," Dahlia said.

"I'm nothing. I'm bored." I could feel my face turning red.

Margo began to laugh.

Next to a periodicals chart, a couple was dancing. They linked arms and dipped into and away from each other, smiling as if they meant it, which I suppose they did. Her velvet pants swirled about her legs, his jacket lapels flapped. Then he reached for her and lifted her above his head and began to twirl around and around and of course he dropped her, and that thud, the dead weight of it, its graceless determinacy, was an embarrassment to the evening. The girl made a sound like *ughhhna*. She was popular and bold, a photographer whose camera perched on the windowsill. Someone seized it and took her picture. Someone else took off her shoes— red Chinese slippers embroidered with mocking birds—and placed them on her head and took another picture. I left after that. The front porch was empty save for some sand-filled flowerpots in which cigarettes had been extinguished, and a Ping-Pong paddle mounded with shaving cream.

I wondered what made the clacking sound that shaving cream cans made, and if the sound grew louder as the can grew emptier. I wondered why Dahlia seemed to enjoy herself at these parties so much more than Margo did. When I'd announced that I was leaving, Margo had nodded in exhausted understanding, but Dahlia had given me an impertinent little wave. Her diffidence must mask a real yearning to be around people, while Margo was too practical to imagine a world in which she could be lonely. It just never occurred to her.

I walked home slowly. The college grounds were teeming with shadowy figures. Someone jumped up onto the railing of a pedestrian bridge and gesticulated wildly. Others were sunk together deep in laughter, like animals tearing at the same meat. During the day it would have been different, the grass would have cried out too brightly and the sunshine would have unmade our anonymity. But at night everyone was alone, whether they knew it or not.

When we told Margo what we were planning to do, she placed an olive in her mouth and worked the flesh away from the pit. "I can tell you right now what the ceremony's going to be like. A comic book." She spat into her hand. "You won't know where to look first."

I was sure this appealed to Dahlia. "What's important is that I inform you of the proceedings, that your feelings don't get hurt," I said.

"Why would my feelings be hurt by seeing my ex-boyfriend cavorting around with my roommate?"

"I don't know."

"Susan, have you ever been in love?" Margo asked.

We were in the kitchen. Margo's plastic container of olives sat on the counter with the lid next to it. The olives glistened, maroon, in their oily brine.

"Love comes from blindness, friendship from knowledge," I answered.

"I suppose that's a no," Margo said.

Dahlia opened the refrigerator and took a swig of ginger ale straight from the bottle. She burped resolvedly. "Where is Sam right now?"

Margo looked at her watch. "He's in class. He gets out at 11:50 and then he goes to the club to have lunch."

"Good. That's where I'll meet him." She pulled on a pair of black boots.

They drooped around her ankles like a small child's stockings.

"Today's Wednesday," Margo called after her. "They'll be having watery minestrone!"

The front door slammed. Silence. A rearrangement of senses, the sort of pause that always accompanied such a thing. I didn't know where to look. The day's instructions, the rules by which one lived, seemed suddenly inaccessible.

Then Margo said, "Sam enjoys portraying himself."

"Do you think he's good at it?"

"His whole life's been spent in study. He used to freeze in front of the bathroom mirror, and make a face, and say, 'That's what bafflement looks like.' Or, 'Therein lies major regret.'"

"But is he any *good?*"

"None of them are. Not a single member. They're mysteries inside, unapproachable. They know themselves only as replicas."

"Have you ever told him that?" I asked.

"Of course not."

"You have to realize that other people can't always tell what you're thinking."

"I depend on it," she said.

I first met Margo and Dahlia in an archeology class. On a warm October morning we took a bus into the Virginia countryside, past horse farms and little churches and barns that looked like they'd been pried open with a crowbar. The fields and leaves were the yellow of sheets hung on a clothes-line—a light-struck, light-stiffened color. Our bus passed a bicyclist in a slicker pedaling furiously down Route 29. It wasn't raining. His slicker-wearing in the sunshine struck me as foolish, and hopeful, in its prepared-ness. We stopped on the outskirts of Colonial Williamsburg and paced off the parameters of the dig, tying twine to wooden stakes and making a rec-tangle. "Go forth and find things," the professor said. A redheaded woman (Margo) was the first to step inside the twine lines. It was as if she were entering a real place, a country guided by some delicate anarchy, and had to act very quickly. She eschewed brushes and worked with her bare hands. The rest of us unearthed bullets but she discovered part of a pewter jug, and when she labeled and bagged it I saw her slip something else into her

pocket. The trees were high and bright and seeing that small theft gave me a feeling of freedom. On the way back to Charlottesville I sat next to her and asked her what she'd taken, but she wouldn't acknowledge my question until we were on campus walking away from the rest of the class. She looked over her shoulder to make sure we weren't being followed. Dahlia was right there. Margo beckoned her to fall in line with us and then drew out of her pocket a mesh ball on a chain. It looked like a tea strainer, but Margo said it was a pendant for filling with herbs and potions and casting spells.

"The colonists would grind anise and sage and burdock root, and place it in the pendant with gloved hands. They believed that if the potion came into contact with skin, the strength of the spell was sapped."

"They practiced witchcraft?" I asked.

"The women did," she said. "They saw it as their duty to keep the peace and allow the proper people to fall in love with each other."

"Historically, women were always doing things like that," Dahlia said.

"Like what?" I was annoyed by how close to me she was walking.

"Molding societies. Being deft shaping forces."

"She's right," Margo said.

We gossiped about our professor and the other students in the class as we walked the rest of the way to our dorms, which ended up being arranged in the same pattern as we were on the sidewalk—Margo's on the end, mine in the middle, and Dahlia's on the other side—and at the end of that semester we left them and rented an apartment together.

Have I ever told you this? I imagined myself asking Margo. Once, I fell asleep to my radio and when I woke up Sam was dancing in my bedroom. His eyes were rolled back in his head and he was bouncing up and down on his toes. I pretended that I was still sleeping. He was wearing cut-off corduroys and a T-shirt with a botanical rendering of poison ivy on it. His skin was as dense and pale as marble. It was the middle of the day. Have I ever told you this?

No, I imagined her answering. But when I say you weird Sam out I mean there is something obstreperous about you, something that refutes what it sees and argues incessantly with the world. You are the kind of person who has to be convinced of simple things, persuaded, dragged forth. You are an admonishment to ease.

Me: That doesn't explain what Sam was doing in my bedroom.

Margo: He was there to fluster you.

Me: He thought I was asleep!

Margo: No, he didn't.

But I never mentioned the incident to her, because I knew she'd have some way of making it a joke on me. Sam had a scar on his jaw from a skiing accident—Margo had struck him accidentally with one of her poles—and as he danced it gleamed, hook-shaped. His breathing was staccato and his chest was like a birdcage whose curved door shuddered outward, shuddered outward but never quite unlatched. As if it contained something too large for itself. He bounced around for a few minutes and then darted from the room. I didn't know whether to laugh. Should I laugh? I asked his departing back. What were your intentions?

When Dahlia returned home after she'd gone to find Sam, I had to fight the urge to immediately ask her what happened. She needed some autonomy, to feel she was an equal partner in the operation. On the other hand, we only had a few days before the ceremony.

She brought a bag of baby carrots and a jar of peanut butter into the living room, where I was taking notes from a psychology textbook. Everyone else I knew toted along something to read while they ate, but not Dahlia. She dipped carrots in the peanut butter and took vigorous bites, staring faultlessly into space.

"If people are waiting in two lines, one markedly longer than the other," I said, "did you know that a test subject will stand at the end of the longer line if the person in front of him does so too?"

"Confusion happens easily," she said.

I closed my book. "Does it?"

"Sam was very eager to talk about Margo. Their relationship was troubled, despite what we thought of it. That time Margo hit him in the face with her ski pole? He thinks it was deliberate. He'd cut her off on a run, and he said she aimed her body at him before she fell and flung her pole through the air."

I wasn't surprised. I could imagine doing all sorts of frustrated, covert things if I were in a relationship with someone like Sam. Someone whose privilege just begged to be undermined. "Where did you two talk?" I asked.

Dahlia began to unravel her braid. "In his room."

"That cesspool?"

"He keeps things very neat. He's got a pencil holder shaped like Vincent van Gogh, and a jar of hard candies on his bookshelf."

"The authority you bring to this subject is quite remarkable, Dahlia," I said.

"Well, of course I'm going to remember the jar of candies," she said. "I was about to eat one when he kissed me." She withdrew from her pocket a half-wrapped butterscotch. The wrapper was sort of sheared away, as if it had come up against a great and roaring passion.

"This is ridiculous," I said, though I could not have explained why. I'd wanted the challenge, but maybe not the victory. Seeing my plan unfold was a way of glimpsing the future, and in doing so I realized how unnatural an act that was. There are certain barriers, I thought, shields smooth as silk, that aren't meant to be perforated. Time was one of those.

"You are the matchmaker," Dahlia reminded me.

"I know," I said ruefully. "I'm in it now."

As I rode my bicycle downtown, its chain rattling, I wondered where the man in the rain slicker had been going that day I saw him from the bus window, the day of the archeology class outing. I hadn't thought about him in over a year, but I could still see his bent billowing figure, his spinning legs. Despite all his effort, the bus had overtaken him easily. Its speed seemed monstrous in retrospect, and the man's endeavoring pure and doomed. Once our bus had passed him he'd been surrounded by a new fleet of vehicles, and I'd lost sight of him before I wanted to.

I locked my bike to a parking meter and went into a clothing store full of circulating undergraduates. Dahlia already had lots of frocks, mostly vintage, sun-faded things, but I figured she could use something new for the Re-enactors' ceremony. The material of the dresses I examined clung together like butterflies caught in the same net. They were brilliant, bound for spacious closets and dabbings of lemon and fizzy water should they become stained. "Does this dress convey a spunky moneyed imperturbability?" I imagined someone asking a saleslady. Dahlia and I were approximately the same height but she was thinner than me. I chose a pale green dress with a scooped neckline, tried it on, and paid for it with a check.

Margo was sitting on the curb in front of the store. She must have followed me there. She took off her headphones, letting them encircle her

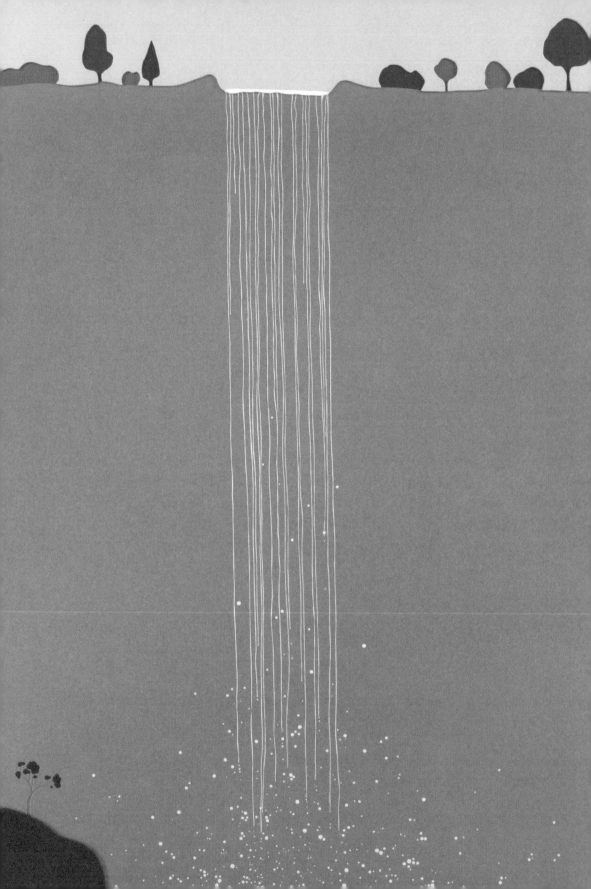

neck, and stood to extend her hand. "Here." She pried open my palm. "You deserve this. It didn't work for me."

The pendant was stuffed with something odorous. "What do you mean?"

"I tried to set Sam and Justine up. But nothing happened." Justine did maintenance for our apartment building, tending to running toilets and sniffing out gas leaks on stoves.

"Justine is a married Southeast Asian woman of indeterminate age," I said.

"All the same," replied Margo, "the power of the pendant is dwindling." She sighed deeply. "When I used to imagine my college years, they were certainly not tinged by such inconsequentiality."

"You're important to your friends."

"Friends? You mean conspirators? You and Dahlia possess a curiosity that is both idle and ravaging." Margo shook her head. "Yet without it, where would you be?"

The sidewalk sparkled with whatever made cement sparkle.

"Nowhere?" I asked.

"Farther away than that," she said.

The night of the ceremony, Dahlia put on the pale green dress and waited for Sam in her bedroom. I was downstairs with Margo. It was raining, and I walked over to the window. The streetlights seemed to concentrate and isolate the downpour, as if their cylindrical heads were rain clouds. When Sam pulled up in an old gray Mercedes, an aristocratic cast-off of his father's, I was sure he would honk. Instead, he came inside.

"Sam!" Margo said. She was sitting on the couch with a Scrabble board spread out on the coffee table in front of her, her expression tender and remonstrative. "You look nice tonight."

Sam shrugged. He was wearing a tuxedo shirt and a pair of pinstriped pants. His eyes were flecked with color, like small aquariums. "You do too."

"Oh good! I'm glad we've established that we both look nice," Margo said.

"Don't be mad, Margo."

"You're going to forget all about me, aren't you?"

"Of course not," Sam said.

"That's funny, because I'm going to forget you," Margo said. "I'm going to forget you forever." Her voice caught, as if there were a carpeted step in her throat.

"Forget you forever? Did you leave out a few ever*s*? Forever and ever and ever, isn't that what you mean?" I said nervously. I was trying to elicit a laugh, but she remained silent and then Dahlia came downstairs. Margo leaped up and with exaggerated deference attempted to drape a raincoat over her shoulders. Dahlia refused it, pushing her away hard enough to cause her to thump her head against the wall—it seemed to bounce—and slide down into a sitting position.

Sam looked distraught. "I am not equipped to have two women pounding themselves into a pulp over me," he said.

"Not *over* you Sam, not *over* you," Margo said from the floor.

I turned to stare at Dahlia. Where had this fierceness come from? She looked as defiant and wild as a runway model, someone who had been powdered with white and arranged in artful rags, but who still retained the structure of beauty. "I think you should go now," I said. "Have a good time."

When I was just a child, I'd seen my mother approach the bathroom where my father was taking a bath with a carton of orange juice in her hand. Although she shut the door behind her, I heard him exclaim as she poured the cold juice in. I was reminded now of the way antipathy between two people created a kind of alternate room in which the others, if there were others, found themselves stranded. But of course, in the case of Margo and Dahlia, I'd built that room myself.

Sam shook loose the folds of his umbrella and prodded Dahlia forward with its tip.

When I woke the next morning I knew right away that Dahlia hadn't returned from the ceremony and that I'd have to go get her. The apartment was very still and shadowed and expectant. Margo was asleep on the couch with her mouth open, not slackly but poised on some defamation. Outside, the pavement was damp from last night's rain.

What can I do? I thought the whole way to the club. I'd never been there alone before. I came with nothing and was looking for something. I came with nothing.

The bushes in front of the large brick building were decorated with paper flowers. Inside, I found the members drinking mimosas. They greeted me with elaborate courtesy. "Good morning, Susan," they said. "Have a croissant, have something to drink." They surrounded me, forcing me backwards, deeper and deeper into the chambers, as if I were being carried along by a wave whose strength I had underestimated. They possessed a tangled innocence, a gravelly purity. A little stubble sat softly on their faces. The Grouper approached me.

"Delighted," he said.

"Tell me where Sam and Dahlia are."

"They're rejoicing."

"In what?"

"In the rejoicing room."

I realized he was drunk. "You're no help at all."

"Listen, we're all here to have a good time. Why aren't you, Susan? Why aren't you ever here to have a good time?"

"I don't know," I said.

"Clearly not." The Grouper sniffed.

I looked at him closely. "What's your real name?"

"Timothy. No! It's buried," he said. "It's gone now."

I backed away, stumbling over a pocketbook. Its clasp was fastened but the leather body was ripped open. A packet of condoms and a little ivory fan, like the calcified tail of a peacock, spilled out onto the floor. "Dahlia," I yelled, "we're surrounded by heathens!"

"She won't hear you," the Grouper said.

"Come get me!" I continued to howl. The Grouper grasped my shoulders and forced me to sit on a couch dusty with pool chalk, and then he left. Across the room, someone had written DUCT TAPE on the wall with duct tape. A chandelier hung at a rakish angle from a wire in the ceiling. Sam appeared.

He sat next to me. His tuxedo shirt was half undone, the frills flattened and sides spread, making a deep V of his skin. The V of migratory birds, an ordered and celestial thing, knowable, unknowable. He appeared suddenly very lovely.

"I thought I might find you here," he said.

"Really? I was looking for *you*." I'd forgotten, in an instant, that it was Dahlia I'd come for.

He leaned toward me and took my hand and it felt nice, steady yet

searching. "Sam, what happened at the ceremony last night?" I asked.

"We just quoted each other and drank cocktails," he said. "That's all we do around here."

I'd expected more than a group of winsome-looking people standing around and pretending to be refined, then devolving gratifyingly, inexorably, into their usual strewn selves. I'd thought members might have recreated for the girlfriends in question moments of love's recognition, capture, containment. "What?" I said. "No chants or incantations, no special rituals?"

"No, just special punch with special vodka." He began to laugh, and his scar shone again. I waited for him to say something else. I wanted him to keep holding my hand in that articulate, grasping way. Instead, he stood and tugged at it.

I followed.

Dahlia wasn't upstairs. She wasn't anywhere I could see. I could see. The pencil holder, the jar of candies, a bunk bed whose lower mattress had been turned on end and propped against the top bunk, creating a slide like a person would use to escape from an airplane—all of this was very clear to me, resonant, fingered, gone over again and again, already a memory. I could see myself lying on Sam's bed with him so close to the ceiling, kissing as if we were mouthing words, speaking with crushed deliberateness. Undressing, hands running over each other's bodies, temporary acts set against a permanent backdrop. Tinfoil stars pinned to the actual sky.

The sound of my own breathing admonished me. We finished. Sam flicked his boxers, which were patterned with cheerleaders resting bullhorns against their bare stomachs, to the floor. "I don't think I'll ever get dressed again," he said.

"That's how I feel every morning," I said.

"Sated?"

"Unwilling."

He smiled. "Oh, dark queen! You make me shiver."

"Margo represented your feelings differently."

"Of course she did."

Margo. Dahlia. Sam. Now me. I felt sick in a very tangible away, as if from food poisoning. I dressed quickly.

"Don't go," he said.

"Why not?"

"Because you could do a cheer for me."

I'd have abandoned myself to his company, had he given me a good reason.

Downstairs. I passed members still drinking in the anteroom, their tousled heads bent over their cups. They were like a field of sheep glimpsed from a touring car's window—matching, remote creatures who simply did what they were meant to do. Outside, the paper flowers were bleeding onto the bushes. When I turned to look back at the club I thought I saw a pale green smudge in an upstairs window. "Dahlia?" I called one last time.

Margo was sitting on the couch in her pajamas when I got home. The toilet flushed. Dahlia walked out of the bathroom.

"How did you beat me home?" I asked.

"I ran," she said.

I sat next to Margo and leaned my head back. I'd wanted to peer into the club's secret workings. I'd wanted to know, to occupy a forbidden space with my knowledge. I'd wanted so many things. Something in me felt faded and abstruse, like ancient writing. Indecipherable. Indecipherable. Have you ever been in love? Margo had asked me. Of course I had. I'd moved from its quiet core to the frayed edge, and beyond, where there were only scraps.

Finally, Margo spoke to both of us. Her hair was pulled back with the kind of low-grade rubber band that came wrapped around free newspapers. "Tell me this," she said. "What do you know now that you didn't before?"

"Everything," I said.

"Enough," Dahlia said. She'd always been the honest one.

We drove out to the chain restaurants on the edge of town then, to get doughnuts or pizza or something else cheap to eat. On our way there, passing a car dealership whose rows of vehicles stretched a parking lot far and wide, I said, "Look at that!"

"What?" Margo and Dahlia asked, a lazy response, because *what* was right in front of them. The cars were blinking. Their hazard lights were on, blinking all at once, and the longer they did so the more in accordance they grew until it appeared that they were perfectly synchronized. The lights were crisp and red and seemed to possess multiply a single vibrant intent. We were moving slowly in a line of traffic and then we stopped. "It's like they're timed," Margo said, reverently.

"Like they've got life," I said.

"*Got life?*" She pounced, someone whose vision had been disturbed. "You mean *alive?*"

I'd had a vision too. "No, like they've *got life*," I insisted. An artificial state, a temporary and uncanny endowment. Beautiful cars.

"They'll become scattered again," Dahlia said, and she was right. The pattern shifted, became variegated, soft. Like Morse code for the deaf, little messages sewn with electric thread. Traffic started moving again. We left the flickering behind.

CONTRIBUTORS

TONY D'SOUZA is a recipient of a 2006 NEA fellowship in prose. His stories have appeared in *The New Yorker, Stand, Black Warrior Review, The Literary Review, Tin House, Playboy,* and elsewhere. His first novel, *Whiteman,* was released by Harcourt in April. He served three years in the Peace Corps, in West Africa, and currently lives in Sarasota, Florida.

AARON GWYN is the author of *Dog on the Cross: Stories* (Algonquin Books), a finalist for the 2005 New York Public Library's Young Lions Award. Algonquin will release his novel, *Ink,* next year. Gwyn's fiction has appeared in *New Stories from the South, Glimmer Train, Black Warrior Review, Indiana Review,* and other magazines. He lives in Charlotte, North Carolina.

BEN JAHN is working toward an MA at UC Davis and on a book of stories called *North of What Matters.* Recently, he won a small grant to study taxidermy. His stories have appeared in *ZYZZYVA, The Greensboro Review,* and in an anthology called *Sierra Songs & Descants.*

ROY KESEY was born in California, and currently lives in Beijing with his wife and children. His fiction and creative nonfiction have appeared in more than forty magazines, including *The Georgia Review, Other Voices, Quarterly West,* and *Maisonneuve.* A novella of his, called "Nothing in the World," won the Bullfight Press Little Book Prize, and was published in May of 2006.

SAM MILLER lives in Atlanta, where he works for the government by night and pursues his Master's degree at Georgia State University by day.

KEVIN MOFFETT's collection of stories, *Permanent Visitors,* won the Iowa Short Fiction Award and will be published in October. His fiction has appeared in *The Oxford American,* and is forthcoming in *The Best American Short Stories 2006.*

JACK PENDARVIS is the author of two books of short stories, *The Mysterious Secret of the Valuable Treasure* and the forthcoming *Your Body is Changing.* His work has appeared in the *Pushcart Prize Anthology,* and he is a frequent contributor to *Paste.*

SARAH RAYMONT lives in New York.

ANTHONY SCHNEIDER has been published in *Bold Type, The Reading Room, Mid-American Review, The Believer, US News & World Report,* and the anthologies *The Literary Insomniac* and *The Encyclopedia of Exes.* He lives without fishes, cats, or a dog in New York.

SUSAN STEINBERG is the author of the story collections *The End of Free Love* and *Hydroplane.* Her stories have appeared in *Conjunctions, Boulevard, The Gettsburg Review,* and elsewhere. She teaches at the University of San Francisco, and is the fiction editor of *Pleiades.*

J. ERIN SWEENEY's stories have appeared in journals including *Hayden's Ferry Review, New Letters, Spork, Cimarron Review,* and *Confrontation.* Her work has also been performed on stage in Carnegie Hall and other venues. She has an MFA from the University of Utah and lives in Philadelphia.

CORINNA VALLIANATOS's fiction has appeared in *Noon, Epoch,* and *A Public Space.*

ROD WHITE, a real estate developer living in Atlanta, received an MFA in fiction writing from the University of Utah. His poetry, short stories, and short plays have appeared in various magazines, including *The Quarterly* and *The Chattahoochie Review.*

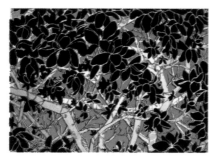

4. Rachel Salomon

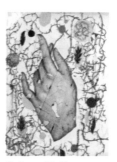

8. Jason Holley

12. Fred Tomaselli

16. Ashley Macomber

20. Amy Cutler

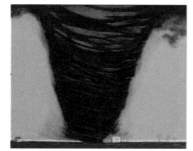

24. Niklas Eneblom

28. Echo Eggebrecht

32. Franz Ackermann

36. Keith Andrew Shore

40. Kevin Christy

44. Holly Coulis

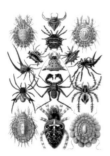

48. Jacob Magraw-Mickelson

52. Mamma Andersson

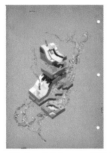

56. Ernst Haeckel

60. Chris Duncan

64. Anonymous

68. Echo Eggebrecht

72. Jason Holley

76. Jules de Balincourt

80. Håvard Homstvedt

84. Ashley Macomber

88. Anna Conway

92. Henri Rousseau

96. Kevin Christy

100. Wendy Heldmann

104. Franz Ackermann

108. Tracy Maurice

112. Andrew Schoultz

116. Susan Logoreci

120. Fred Tomaselli

124. Keith Andrew Shore

128. Jodie Mohr

132. Andrew Schoultz

136. Anna Conway

140. Håvard Homstvedt

144. Kuniyoshi Utagawa

148. Jules de Balincourt

152. Angelina Guladoni

156. Susan Logoreci

160. Jodie Mohr

164. Kent Henricksen

168. Clare Rojas

172. Wendy Heldmann

176. Angela Dufresne

180. Rachel Salomon

184. Rachell Sumpter

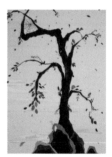

188. Laura Owens

192. Jeff Gauntt

196. Niklas Eneblom

200. Henri Rousseau

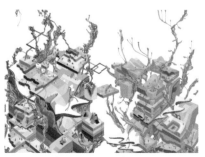

Cover. Jacob Magraw-Mickelson

CREDIT INFO

If there is an 826 Writing Lab in your city, state, or time zone,

PLEASE GET INVOLVED.

You'll be glad you did.

www.826valencia.org
826 Valencia St.
San Francisco, CA

www.826nyc.org
372 5th Ave.
Brooklyn, NY

www.826la.org
685 Venice Blvd.
Venice, CA

www.826chi.org
1331 North Milwaukee Ave.
Chicago, IL

www.826michigan.org
2245 South State St., Suite 100
Ann Arbor, MI

www.826seattle.org
8414 Greenwood Ave.
North Seattle, WA